HEARTS OF TRUST

SEARCHING HEARTS

BOOK THREE

ELLIE ST. CLAIR

Facebook: Ellie St. Clair

Cover by AJF Designs

Do you love historical romance? Receive access to a free ebook, as well as exclusive content such as giveaways, contests, freebies and advance notice of pre-orders through my mailing list!

Sign up here!

Also By Ellie St. Clair

Searching Hearts
Duke of Christmas (prequel)
Quest of Honor
Clue of Affection
Hearts of Trust
Hope of Romance
Promise of Redemption

Searching Hearts Box Set (Books 1-5)

For a full list of all of Ellie's books, please see
www.elliestclair.com/books.

CONTENTS

PROLOGUE

*J*t was the sneeze that gave him away.

He hadn't counted on the dust that had accumulated behind the drapes, where he hid in his father's study. Of course, nine-year-old Benjamin didn't realize the sun behind him completely illuminated his figure, and his father was choosing to play along with the game.

"I say, is someone there?" boomed Lionel Harrington, the Duke of Ware. Hardly any of his peers would recognize the duke as he was in these moments with his children.

Benjamin clapped a hand over his mouth to keep from laughing.

"Is there an intruder in my study?" the duke asked, pretending to search under his impressive Chippendale desk, behind the leather chairs, and in the empty fireplace.

Finally he threw back the curtains, his son erupting into giggles at his discovery. "Ho, look here! Whatever shall I do with you, boy?" Lionel lifted him up and swung him around the room, sending Benjamin into fits of glee.

"Now," continued the duke, setting Benjamin on his lap, "Where are your brothers and sisters?"

"Daniel, Thomas, and Violet are with the governess," Benjamin said, then stopped abruptly as he realized he was providing far too much information.

"Yet you do not have to do any learning today?"

"No," Benjamin replied, shaking his head vigorously.

"And Polly, she also does not have to sit with the governess?" At his question, the duke heard a noise from the corner of the room. "For if you both have escaped the woman, your mother will be quite vexed. You know this is the third governess she has hired this year."

"Yes, Father, we know."

"Be good, children," the duke said, before rising from his seat on the arm of the chair.

"Father?" Benjamin's voice rose in question as he tugged at his sleeve.

"Yes, son?"

"Mama says that Daniel has to work hard at his lessons because he is to be a duke himself one day. Violet and Polly need to learn in order to be 'polished young ladies who will find a good match.' But what about Thomas and me? Are we going to make good matches one day too?"

The duke knelt down so that he could look into his son's face.

"Yes, I do hope you find a good match one day, 'tis true," he said with a nod. "However, you and Thomas can both do anything in life you please."

"Can I be a duke?"

Lionel chuckled. "I suppose you cannot do *anything*, for no, you cannot likely be a duke. You can be part of the army, you can go into the clergy, you can be a barrister... why, there are many options."

"Would it be all right if I just had fun every day playing for the rest of my life?"

The duke smiled at his son and ruffled his hair before

they heard a shrill voice calling. "Oh, dear," he said. "You best get out of here before the governess finds you or your mother sees you. She'll want you at your lessons. Polly, out from behind the bookshelf now, return to your studies."

"Yes, Father," she said contritely, appearing from the corner of the room. She joined Benjamin as they raced from the study, the duke smiling after them.

This was what life was all about.

CHAPTER 1

FIFTEEN YEARS LATER

*B*enjamin Harrington, third son to the Duke of Ware, groaned loudly as the curtains in his bedchamber were thrown open. A stream of sunlight hit him across the face, making his head burn with pain.

"Close those!" he barked, throwing his arm across his eyes to block out the light. "What do you think you are doing? I shall have you dismissed!"

The maid, however, was used to the bluster that accompanied him when he woke and ignored his orders. Instead, she placed the breakfast tray on the small table by the roaring fire and left the room, clearly not in the least bit concerned over Benjamin's threats.

Muttering under his breath, Benjamin wondered whether he had enough energy to get out of bed and close the drapes himself before crawling back under the covers, or if he was best to simply deal with the fact that he had been awakened for a reason and was obviously expected. The maid had evidently been following his mother's orders, given how she had ignored his instructions, which meant that there would be consequences if he did not rise from his bed.

And if his mother had given strict instructions to the maid, then she would certainly report to his father if he did not appear soon after being awakened.

Groaning out of frustration rather than pain, Benjamin dropped his arm back to his side and tried to open his eyes. He blinked in the sunlight and squeezed his eyes tightly shut for a few moments until he ventured to open them again.

Throwing back the bed linens and quilt, he walked across the cold wooden floor to the fire, dressed only in his night-shirt. How he'd had the presence of mind to change out of his clothes last night, he could not say, for he had imbibed a great deal of liquor. Most likely his valet, the ever-faithful Peter, had waited up to assist him, although Benjamin could not even remember climbing the stairs to his room. It must have been a damned good evening if he could not recall a thing about it.

His stomach churned, but Benjamin drank the coffee and ate his toast regardless, knowing that, even though he wanted to refuse ant food or drink, it would help the ache in his head. By his second cup, Benjamin was beginning to feel a little better and he sat back in his chair with a sigh.

The day was bright, although it looked as though the sun was already beginning to fade. Glancing at the clock, Benjamin was surprised to see that it was already late after-noon – not that the time particularly mattered. He had become a creature of the night of late, spending his days in bed and his nights out with friends, at whatever soiree or ball they could find, and if not there, then at a club or gaming hall. For what else was the third son of a duke to do?

A frown wrinkled his brow. The truth of the matter was that Benjamin had very little idea about what to do with his future. He had no direction, no thought of where to take his next steps. His eldest brother had the title to worry about, of course, and Thomas had joined the Navy, although goodness knows where he was at the present moment. His sister Violet had been forced into a hasty marriage, albeit an apparently happy one, which left him and his sister Polly at home.

Polly's direction in life was to find herself a suitable husband, of course, but Benjamin was not as eager to enter the matrimonial state. It seemed too proper, too much like duty and that was the one thing he did not particularly care for. Duty meant propriety. It meant acting with thought and good sense, and Benjamin was quite enjoying not having to worry about such things. At times, he was perturbed by his lack of future direction, but it was easy to push such thoughts away, especially when there was good liquor and easy women to be enjoyed. Besides, at only four and twenty, he was still a young man with many years ahead of him until he would have to settle down.

There was a scratch at the door. Benjamin called for the person to enter, only for his valet to appear with a slightly apologetic look on his face.

"Forgive me for my tardiness, my lord," he said, hastily walking over toward Benjamin. "I did not know you had awoken."

Benjamin shrugged. "It is of little consequence. I assume my mother wishes to speak to me, so I suppose I must dress."

Peter nodded, walking toward the wardrobe to pick out Benjamin's clothes. Benjamin watched him for a moment, a slightly puzzled expression coming across his face. "Did I come home late last night?"

"You did, my lord," his valet replied, without a hint of censure in his voice. "Accompanied by a young lady."

A jolt ran through him. That was a surprise. He never

brought women home. Not to his family's house. "A lady? Here?"

"Indeed, my lord."

Benjamin ran a hand over his face.

"I did not wake up with anyone beside me," Benjamin murmured, his frown deepening as he tried to recall what had happened. "Are you quite sure?"

"I believe she left in the early hours of the morning," his valet replied, his face expressionless as he laid out Benjamin's clothes. "I came in promptly to rescue your cravat and other such garments." He sighed slightly, apparently displeased with the state of his clothing.

Benjamin tried to remember who it was he had taken to his bed, but his mind conjured up no image of the lady, nor of any pleasures they might have shared. That was more than a little frustrating, but it was, unfortunately, one of the consequences of drinking too much brandy. It was not uncommon for Benjamin to take women to his bed, but he normally had his eye on them for some time beforehand. They had to be just right – women who did not wish for matrimony or the like but were seeking a liaison of sorts. They were often wealthy widows although, at times, Benjamin had occasion to visit some local establishments. Today, however, Benjamin simply had no recollection.

Shrugging off the feeling of unease that settled over him, he decided that there was nothing for it but to ask one of his friends, once he'd listened to whatever it was his mother had to say. He would listen, mumble something as he usually did, and then make his way from the house.

Surely someone would know who this mysterious lady had been? Then again, perhaps she wanted to remain anonymous. The thought made his lips curve into a smile, as he began to look forward to the evening's pleasures. Yes, indeed, life was very good – and he was sure it was only going to get better.

* * *

"Benjamin!"

His mother's voice had him wincing, for his headache hadn't yet disappeared. "Mama, a little more quietly, if you please."

"I will speak as loudly as I wish," she replied, her eyes boring holes into him from where she stood with her arms crossed in the middle of her drawing room, which his brother Thomas, a naval captain, had always jokingly called the helm of her ship. "Now, sit down. I have a great deal to say to you."

With a heavy sigh, Benjamin sat, slumping into an over-stuffed chair as he passed a hand over his eyes, already tired of the situation. Since his older sister had married, his mother had become more focused on him than he would have liked. "If you are going to lecture me, Mama, can you please make it quick? I have plans."

She gaped at him, and he continued in the silence.

"That *is* what you were going to do, was it not?" he said. "To tell me that I must make something of myself, that I must stop my frivolous ways and find something of import to do?" He had heard it all before and was growing weary of the same words being flung at him on a fairly regular occurrence. "I must tell you, Mama, that I have very little inclination to do such a thing, for I am quite happy in my present state."

His mother's eyes glinted with anger, causing the slightest touch of fear within Benjamin. "Your father and I are far from pleased, Benjamin! For goodness sake, the maids are gossiping about the lady who crept from your room in the small hours of the morning. I cannot have such behavior in my house. You are bringing shame to our family."

He shrugged, trying not to let her words affect him. "I am of age to do as I please, Mama."

A slight smile curved her lips, surprising him and making him sit up a bit taller in his chair, suddenly suspicious. This was not the reaction he had expected.

"You forget, Benjamin, that the matter of your father's will is something still to be decided. You believe that you can continue as you please, with nothing to stop you – but I think that you should consider the matter a little more carefully."

He frowned at her, no longer slouching, but sitting forward in alarm. "Father's will? What are you talking about, Mama?"

Benjamin watched her smile widen as she sat down, taking her time to sit carefully and brush the wrinkles from her skirts. He knew she was making him wait and tried his best not to let his frustrations show. "Mama?" he muttered, seeing her eyes on him. "What are you trying to say?"

The smile disappeared and she fixed him with her gaze. "I mean this, Benjamin. Your father has always intended to provide each of you with a sizeable settlement. That can easily be changed."

Staring at her, Benjamin let her words wash over him, trying his best to work out what it was she was suggesting.

"Are you trying to tell me that Father will remove me from his will if I do not 'settle down'?" he asked in carefully measured tones, quite sure that his mother was bluffing.

"That is precisely what I am saying," his mother replied, calmly. "We care for you, Benjamin, but we cannot continue to watch our fortune frittered away on wastefulness as you bring dishonor on yourself, your family, and young ladies."

"It is my money," Benjamin bit out, his collar suddenly a little too tight. "I have money of my own."

"You have *some*," she answered. "But most of what you have is from the good grace of your father. You will need to start being more careful, Benjamin. That money is not going to last forever. Should you continue to fritter through your current finances, you are not guaranteed to have anything else to live on once your father passes away."

Benjamin narrowed his eyes, regarding his mother carefully.

"Father's not... not ill, is he Mama?"

"No, of course not. With any luck he has many years remaining on this earth, however, one never knows. You have been warned, Benjamin."

This was the first time she had made such a threat, and he was not quite sure whether or not he believed her. Was he going to call her bluff and continue with his evening plans regardless? Or was this enough of a threat to force him to do as she asked?

The stubbornness that had always been within him rose to the fore once more, making his jaw clench. "I do not believe you would ever do such a thing, Mama," he said, eventually, getting to his feet. "Your words mean nothing, for they hold no threat." He chuckled then and shook his head, realizing that his father was not even present. "I'd bet you haven't even spoken to Father about such things and have come up with this all on your own, in an attempt to bend me to your will."

"Your disrespect for me is obvious," she said angrily, standing up to face him. "If you do not listen to me, then I shall make sure you listen to your father."

Benjamin shrugged, refusing to listen to her any longer. "Good day, Mama. I shall not be back home until the early hours." He heard her angry monologue begin once more but refused to listen to it, walking from the room. "Don't wait up for me. I do not intend to rush home, not even with your threats hanging over my head." With a chuckle, he pulled the door closed behind him and walked down the stairs to the front door.

CHAPTER 2

Sophie Carmichael sat at the long dining table, pushing around the potatoes and peas on her plate. The dark room that normally echoed was silent, but for the click of utensils. She took a breath as she tried to determine the best way to approach her cousin.

"Malcolm," she began slowly, looking up at the handsome man across the table from her. "I've been thinking."

"Well, that is notable." He looked down his long nose at her with a sneer.

She ignored his barb and continued. "I should like to talk to you about going to London."

"To London?" His face snapped up to meet hers, his steely grey eyes beading as they ran over her, assessing. "Why would you want to go to London?"

"For the season," she said, willing herself not to back down from him. "It is time that I found a husband. Since my parents passed, I have remained in mourning. It has been well over a year now and I feel that I should – "

Her cousin, the Earl of Dunstable, cut her off with a snort. "Sophie, you have everything you need right here in the home I have so generously provided you. I believe I have made my intentions quite clear. As you say, the period of mourning is over, and I am pleased that you have done away with those hideous black dresses of yours. It is time we moved things along. You say you want a husband? I have offered you that and more. That is, once I determine whether you will suit."

He shot a smirk her way. He had been more than clear on how he would assess whether or not she would do as his wife.

Her lecherous distant cousin had begrudgingly taking her in after the death of her parents. At first he was charming and kind, and she had been grateful for all he had done for her. But soon he had turned, showing his true self and deciding that he required payment for residing with him — in the form of her in his bed.

Sophie had been filled with revulsion at the suggestion and had made her stance quite clear – only for his propositions to become more than just words. A few weeks ago, he had managed to get her alone and had pinned her against the wall, attempting to kiss her as he groped at her skirts. Sophie had brought up her knee, and he had doubled over in pain. That had been the day she'd placed her room key on a chain around her neck. With the help of the housekeeper, they had hidden the remainder of the keys to her room, making it the sole place she could be safe.

The chain was delicate and she made sure never to allow her cousin to see it. He had demanded to know where the key was, of course, but she had simply refused to answer – and had then been forced to spend much of her time hiding in her room from his ensuing wrath.

She had been hopeful she could convince him to take her to London where, should she not find a suitable match, she could perhaps find a way to escape from him, taking a position as a governess or some such post.

"Besides, dear cousin," he continued, "how could you be so cruel as to suggest we leave Mother?"

Malcolm's mother lived in the country home with them, providing a sense of propriety to the entire situation. In truth, however, she was fairly ill and seldom left her chambers. Sophie was quite on her own, besides the servants who did all they could to provide her with warnings of her cousin's moods so she was able to distance herself.

"You!" Malcolm's sudden shout at the footman caused Sophie to jump. "Come, refill my glass. Pay attention, boy, to when your lord requires you."

Sophie cringed that her suggestion to Malcolm had roused his anger and Andrew, the footman, was having to deal with it. "Now, Sophie," he continued, his mood flipping to one of smiles and charm. "Once we are finished, will you be ready to depart for Lady Jamison's ball?"

Sophie felt sick at the thought of arriving on her cousin's arm and conversing with the other guests as if nothing was the matter. Besides that, Lady Jamison's home was some miles away, which would also require a carriage ride of some length with her cousin.

"I'm afraid I am feeling quite unwell, Malcolm," she said, not untruthfully. "Would you mind so much if I stayed behind tonight?"

"Suit yourself," he said with a shrug as he tossed back the full glass Andrew had poured for him. "See, I told you, Sophie, this house is where you are comfortable and this is where you shall remain."

She nodded and rose to escape him. "Goodnight, then, Malcolm," she said, and made for the door. She was nearly there when he shot out of his chair and with surprising speed and grace blocked her exit, backing her against the wall.

"Now, Sophie," he said with a leer, "just be sure to be a good girl and wait up for me, will you? No hiding yourself away behind your locked door tonight."

He leaned down toward her, but she managed to dodge his lips and slip out of the confines of his arms, making her way up the stairs as fast as she could as his laugh followed her, sending shivers of fear and revulsion down her spine.

For so long she had assumed he was merely toying with her, but with each passing day she could feel that he was coming closer to acting on his threats.

She waited in her room, listening for him to leave as she sat in front of the well-built fire, reveling in the warmth it threw, the heat seeping through her chilled frame. The chill was, in fact, less due to the temperature of the room and more so because of the strain of her entire situation. She had to find a way to leave this place, to fend for herself.

With all her heart, she wished her mother and father still lived. They had been kind and loving, never once regretting that she, their long-awaited lone child, was not a male heir. They'd lived quietly and simply, even though her father had been a viscount. He had never thrown his wealth and title around but had chosen to live well within their means.

Sophie had grown up enjoying the outdoors instead of balls and soirees. Even though she had been blessed with one season in London, she had not particularly enjoyed it. Her mother and father had been whispering about securing her marriage to a young, unattached titled gentleman in the next county. Upon hearing the description of the man, Sophie had become open to the idea – but all that had come to naught the moment her parents had left this earth.

Their death had been a tragic one, although not unheard of. A carriage accident over a steep, rocky hillside that had ended in their death.

Mourning the loss of both parents had been heart-wrenching and, to this day, Sophie was not quite over the absence of them from her life. How much had changed since then. The will had handed over her father's estate to a distant cousin, the Earl of Dunstable, with the promise that he would then care for Sophie until she found a husband of her own. Her father's fortune was tied up in her matrimony. When she was married, the wealth would be settled on her as a dowry.

Of course, that left Sophie with very little of her own funds and at first she had thought of Malcolm, her cousin, as something of a savior. He had welcomed her to live at his estate much grander than her previous home, to where he now would not let her return. He had encouraged her to settle in and had given her the space and time she needed to mourn. However, it was as if he had grown impatient with her, and had begun to press his attentions onto her after only a few months, insisting that she must come to his bed and he would, in time, marry her.

At first, Sophie could not understand it and had rebuffed him easily enough. Although Malcolm was a handsome man, there was something behind his eyes that prevented her from ever truly trusting him – and, as far as she was concerned, you could not have a marriage if there was no trust to be had. All she could trust in was his thirst for her dowry.

She was becoming desperate to find a way out. But how?

CHAPTER 3

"What do you mean, you don't know who she was?"

Benjamin grinned as one of his friends stared at him, aghast. "Just that. The butler insists that I had a lady beside me last night but, for the life of me, I simply cannot recall who that particular lady was."

"Typical," his friend Lord Murton muttered. "You are far too good-looking, Harrington. That is your problem."

A chuckle went around the group before the men continued discussing the lady's possible identity. Benjamin only half listened, his deep blue eyes idly roving across the dance floor and the guests surrounding it.

He knew that he cut a somewhat dashing figure, and had been blessed with his father's strong features and dark straight hair. It was quite true that, despite his lack of title, the ladies he sought attention from did not turn him away and he had to laugh at Lord Murton's envious comment. Apparently, the man had not had a warm body in his bed for some time.

Benjamin, taken by surprise, let his gaze drift to Lady Anna. This was the lady he had taken to his bed? An untried, unwed, debutante? When had he become so stupid?

"You attempted to lay with her," Lord Simons continued, his voice now shaking with anger. "Thankfully, you were too much in your cups to do anything other than fall asleep, but that does not take away from the shame you have placed on my daughter's shoulders."

"And you know all this because she told you?" Lord Penn interjected, lifting his brows.

Lord Simons nodded, his eyes never leaving Benjamin. "She has told me everything and I am here to demand retribution."

"You want her to marry Harrington?" Lord Penn asked, laughter in his voice. "Harrington, who is well known to be a rake and a wastrel?" He shook his head as Benjamin shot him a look. "Come now, Lord Simons, be reasonable. Even if what you are saying is true, your daughter deserves better than Harrington."

Benjamin inwardly cringed, his gut twisting as he saw the girl begin to cry all over again. "You say that I did not touch her?" he asked, quietly, seeing the man give a sharp nod. "Then I will be truthful with you, Lord Simons, and say that I have no recollection of your daughter's company last evening, and, in addition to this, what Lord Penn says is quite correct – I am not a good choice for a husband." He managed a wry smile, seeing Lord Simons grow a little confused. "What other retribution would you seek?"

Lord Penn grinned, leaning back lazily against the wall. "Lord Simons, does anyone else know of your daughter's late-night excursion?"

"Well, the servants," the man muttered, slowly stepping away from Benjamin. "Given that she did appear back at the house in a state of disarray, having had to walk from your home to our own townhouse in the early hours of the morning."

Something slammed into Benjamin's gut as he took in the girl's pale features, her cheeks still damp from her shed tears. He had never meant to do something as foolish as this and continuing to deny it was only increasing his guilt. Should someone discover what she had done, then her reputation would be well and truly ruined, whereas he would continue to do just as he pleased, unhindered by rumor and gossip. Suddenly, his mother's words came back to haunt him, adding to his burden of guilt. *You are bringing shame to our family.*

"Lord Simons … Lady Anna," he said, lowering his gaze for a moment. "I am truly sorry if what you say is true. I do not lie when I tell you I was heavily in my cups last evening and cannot recall a single thing that took place."

"That is – "

Benjamin held up one hand, silencing Lord Simons' outburst. "Please, my lord," he said, quietly. "What I was to say is that you are quite right in looking for some kind of retribution, but I do not think that a hasty marriage is the right idea, given my reputation."

Lord Simons eyes glittered but he did not object. "Then what do you suggest?"

"Your servants must be told not to gossip, on pain of redundancy," Benjamin said, firmly. "In addition, I shall add what I can to Lady Anna's dowry – discreetly, of course, so that she might find herself a worthy husband." It was not what the man was looking for, he was sure, but Benjamin felt he could do nothing more.

To his very great surprise, Lord Simons did not take long to consider his position, naming an amount of money that made Benjamin wince. It was not an amount he could come

up with on his own, but what else was he to do? He could not exactly refuse, given what he had obviously done, and so a price was agreed upon, hands were shaken, and Benjamin was left wondering how he was meant to explain such a thing to his father.

CHAPTER 4

Sophie put down her book and slowly rose to her feet, her skin turning to ice. She had thought her cousin would be gone for some time, but his voice in the hall, signalled that he had returned far earlier than she had hoped.

Placing her book on the table, she carefully moved to the opposite side of the room, wondering where she could hide herself. Her cousin was determined, if nothing else, and her only true escape would be to hide in her room.

"Sophie? Where are you?"

His sing-song voice was filled with mirth, which made Sophie's heart clench with fright. Malcolm was clearly now drunk, which did not bode well for her. He was always more lecherous when he had taken too much liquor.

Could she make her way to the door and, when he opened it, run past him and escape to her room? It was the only thing that might take him by surprise for, even when he was fully in his cups, Malcolm was still both strong and swift. She did not want to be cornered in the library as, on one previous occasion when he had found her in the drawing room, he had pulled a key from his pocket and proceeded to lock the door in order to prevent her escape.

Thankfully, he had not thought about the smaller door on the left-hand side of the drawing room, and Sophie had managed to escape him without too much difficulty. However, the library only had one entrance, which meant that if he tried to do the same here, then she could easily be trapped.

Her stomach churned as she hurried toward the door, hearing his voice growing closer. Would she manage to escape past him?

I have to, she told herself, determined not to lose her head and give in to the swirling panic. *I have to get away.*

"Reading again, are we?" Malcolm taunted, now just outside the door. "Of course, my fair cousin always has her head in a book!"

Sophie pressed herself against the wall, trying hard not to make a sound. She closed her eyes, forcing her breathing to remain slow and even. Once he entered, the door would hide her from his view, and, when he took a few steps, she would have only a second to rush past him and run toward her room.

The handle slowly began to turn, and, as the door began to open, Sophie held her breath. Her cousin walked in, his steps barely faltering as he moved. However he did it, he was always able to hide the extent of his drunkenness, although his voice usually gave it away. She had seen him imbibe a great deal of liquor and still remain standing, even though his friends had all collapsed across couches and chairs, not even able to lift their heads.

"Sophie?" he called, one hand still on the door handle. "Where are you?"

She had to move. She had to go, now, as he took a step forward and his hand left the handle. Drawing in a quick breath, she moved forward but realized too late she had mistimed her exit and she slammed into him, hard. He stumbled and she heard him grunt as he fell and she hurried out of the room – only for one hand to grab at her ankle.

A shriek left her mouth as she lost her footing, her hands hitting the floor as she tried to keep herself from crashing into it.

"Where do you think you are going so quickly?" Malcolm called out, striking terror into her soul. She knew what he wanted, knew what he intended to do when he got a hold of her. There was no other option but to get away.

His hand was tight around her ankle, but she kicked out with her other foot, hearing a crunch as she connected with something hard. A roar of pain met her ears, but she kicked out again and again, until, finally, he let go of her.

Her soft slippers torn off, she left them behind as she ran in bare feet toward her room, her pulse roaring in her ears. She was quite sure she could hear him running after her, his screams of frustration chasing her down the hall.

Lifting her skirts high, grateful for the simple muslin dress she wore, Sophie climbed the stairs as fast as she could, hearing his insults behind her, growing ever closer. The door to her bedchamber was only a few steps away and, hearing his thumping feet on the stairs, she scrambled for the key she wore around her neck. Her fingers slipped on the metal as she put the key in the lock, turning it quickly. Once it clicked, she wrenched the door open, slipped inside and slammed it shut. Time was slipping away from her as she tried to put the key back in the lock, knowing she had to lock it tightly if she was to be safe. Her fingers were shaking so hard that it took three attempts before the key turned successfully.

A loud thump threw her back from the door, her scream echoing around the room. Terror clutched at her heart as he

banged furiously at her door, the handle rattling as it turned over and over – but, to her relief, the door held.

"Come now, Sophie! You owe this to me, do you not? I deserve this for taking you in and showing you such great affection."

Sophie put her hand against her mouth, willing herself not cry out. His thumps grew louder and more forceful, and the door began to shake. Feeling as if she had to secure the door even further just to be sure he could not break in, Sophie dragged a heavy chair over toward the door, placing it under the door handle. He obviously heard her actions, as his voice grew louder.

"You struck me, Sophie, and I think that should be returned in kind." His voice took on a gravelly tone, sending shudders through her. "Come out now and I swear I will not make it as bad as I was initially intending."

Slowly moving away from the door, Sophie padded toward the fire burning in the grate, glad that there was, at least, some warmth emanating from it. She threw a few more logs on top of the glowing embers and sank down on the crimson wool carpet, draping the skirts of her gown over her toes. She had done this a great many times before, knowing that she had nothing else to do but wait.

Sooner or later, her cousin would give up and leave her alone, although she probably would not emerge from her room until she saw him go out riding the following morning or leave in his carriage. She had thought he had gone out for the evening to Lady Jamison's ball, but he must have returned early without her knowledge. It was her own fault for becoming so engrossed in the book she had been reading.

"You cannot hide forever Sophie," his voice came through. "I'll be waiting — that is a promise."

His heavy footsteps signified his departure, and the trembling that shook Sophie's body slowly began to decrease as she realized that she was safe as she could be for the time being. Her gaze was drawn to something steaming in the corner, her heart warming when she saw the tray. That was the cook's doing, and Sophie could not have appreciated it more. The staff were her only comfort in this life of fear.

Catching a glimpse of herself in the mirror, she appeared a madwoman, brown tendrils of her hair having escaped her usual chignon and curling about the perspiration on her forehead. The bodice of her dress was askew from her fall, and her hazel eyes stared back at her in despair.

She brushed her shaking hands back over her hair, fixed the top of her dress and rose to her feet and made her way over to the tray.

Picking it up, Sophie carried it back to the fire, letting her gaze drift over the teapot and tray of small cakes. The cook must have heard the master come home and had sent up a tray to Sophie's room, knowing she would spend the remainder of the evening in hiding. Sophie was ever so grateful.

She closed her eyes tightly against the rush of tears. She had nothing but this life, no nearby friends or acquaintances, no one she could look to for aid.

She was still in turmoil some hours later, sitting quietly in front of the dying fire, her thoughts all in a muddle. Her tea was cold, the cakes were gone, and she was left with only her own shadow for company. A quiet scratch at the door had Sophie stiffening, only to hear the voice of the cook whispering through the keyhole.

Hurrying to the door, Sophie lifted the key from around her neck and opened the door, as the cook, Mrs. Andrews, stepped inside and shut it behind her, gesturing for Sophie to lock it again.

"He is wandering the hallways, so I had to be careful,"

Mrs. Andrews whispered, her eyes searching Sophie's face. "Are you quite all right, miss?"

Sophie managed a smile. "I am, thank you. And thank you for what you left me."

Mrs. Andrews frowned. "I am only sorry the maid I sent to alert you to the master's presence did not reach you in time."

"That's quite all right," Sophie replied, sitting down by the fire once more. "Are you sure you're safe to come here?"

Sitting opposite Sophie, Mrs. Andrews's face was filled with alarm. "It was important to tell you, Miss Carmichael, that your cousin has called for the local smithy."

"The blacksmith?" Sophie asked, wondering why the lady looked so alarmed. "Whatever for?"

Mrs. Andrews shook her head. "To get a new lock for this room."

Ice washed through her veins. "A new lock?" she whispered, her hands gripping the arms of the chair. "He means to…"

"Yes," Mrs. Andrews finished when Sophie's words trailed off. "He means to have you, my dear, one way or the other. You have never been safe here, but as of tomorrow, you will be completely without refuge."

Sophie's breath hitched. "Tomorrow?" she breathed, her stomach tightening. "The smithy is coming tomorrow?"

"You must leave," Mrs. Andrews said, briskly. "I have come to help you."

"I – I can't," Sophie protested, fear winding its way through her as she looked wildly around the small room that had been both home and prison since she had come to reside in the house. "I have nowhere else to go yet!"

The cook reached across and patted her hand. "I have a sister who works at another estate. I wrote to her – I mean, the housekeeper did, on my behalf, given that I'm not so good with letters – but she knows to expect you. You'll have to stop halfway at an inn, so take whatever coins you have."

Sophie did not know what to say, suddenly overcome by Mrs. Andrews' kindness.

"She will give you a position as a maid. I know it is not nearly the station you were born to," the cook continued. "But at least it will give you time to think about what you can do. You must remain hidden, though. I do not think that cousin of yours will give up on you easily."

"I – I don't know how to thank you," Sophie whispered, tears beginning to gather in her eyes. "Without you and the others, I would have been quite at his mercy by now."

Mrs. Andrews' expression darkened. "He'll get what's coming to him one day, I'm sure of it. But right now, you've got to get yourself away from this place. Come on, dear. I'll help you pack."

CHAPTER 5

*I*t was with a great deal of shame that Benjamin went to speak to his father the day following his conversation with Lord Simons. He wasn't able to meet his father's eye as he confessed all.

He had returned home the night before after the confrontation, and had spent the rest of it turning over every option in his mind, hoping to come up with another way. But it was no use. He needed an advance on the next amount of funds that were due to be deposited in his account in around a month's time and then some, and this actions weighed heavily t on his shoulders.

Finally, he decided that he was best to hold nothing back, but offer the full truth. As he spoke, his father remained quiet, sitting back in his chair and watching Benjamin with eyes sharper than usual.

The man was typically fairly uninterested in the details of their lives, with the exception of their eldest brother, Daniel. He was content with his wife providing guidance to the rest of them. Now, however, his usual nonchalance was replaced with a hard, assessing stare.

Once Benjamin had finished speaking, there was a prolonged silence. Benjamin wished that the ground would open up and swallow him whole.

"Your mother has repeatedly expressed to me her concerns about you," the duke said eventually, disappointment evident in his features, which were so like Benjamin's own. "I told her you would find your way, but appears that, as always, she was right. Only yesterday, she told me how uninterested you were in listening to her words, even though they were wise and true. You showed a lack of respect for your mother and for me when you refused to listen."

"I know," Benjamin said, miserably. The mistakes he had made suddenly brought his life into sharp relief, making him realize just how much of a mess he had made.

"You have lost yourself in a world of pleasure," his father continued, quietly. "It is something that a great many gentlemen do, although most come out the other side with a renewed sense of their responsibilities and a dedication to their work. That, however, has not happened to you. I expect that you might never arrive there on your own, being that you have nowhere to turn."

Benjamin sighed, his eyes on his boots, unable to even look at his father. "I am sorry, Father."

"You need not apologize to me!" he exclaimed, pushing himself up a little straighter in his chair. "Rather, you need to think of that young lady that you brought here. Whether you were inebriated or not, you should know better than to dally with young ladies, Benjamin." When Benjamin finally met his father's eyes, he saw that his face was twisted in pain rather than anger, which only cut deeper into Benjamin's heart. "I think it just as well that Lord Simons chose not to push for you to marry his daughter. It shows that he cares for his daughter, and not just his family's reputation."

His father's words hit Benjamin hard, although he could

not easily dismiss them. "I did not — did not take her innocence, although I am aware I have nearly ruined her. I have said that I am sorry, Father. To the lady and to her father."

"That does not cut it!" his father retorted angrily, banging his fist on his desk in a show of emotion Benjamin was not used to seeing from the man. Benjamin raised his eyes and saw his father gazing at him speculatively before sighing heavily as his shoulders slumped, the anger receding.

"Perhaps it is my fault," the duke said, sadly. "I have not guided you as I ought."

"No, Father," Benjamin replied at once, not wishing for his father to take on the mantle of what was ultimately his own responsibility. "You have tried to give me the time to choose my own path and I confess that I have am beginning to realize I have made rather poor decisions."

His father raised dull eyes to his. "You have no thought of your future, then?"

Biting his lip, Benjamin shook his head, feeling as though he were the biggest disappointment a man could have for a son. He had rarely taken the time to assess his life, as much of it was spent in rather a daze of alcohol and good times.

"Then I have a plan," his father responded, making Benjamin look up in surprise. A sudden chill ran through him as he recalled what his mother had threatened. Was his father about to be cut out from his father's will? Had he gone too far, and was to be cast aside by the family?

"You are to leave this place and go where I tell you," his father continued, firmly. "You are to remain there and make it as profitable as you can."

Confused, Benjamin stared at his father. "Make what profitable, Father?"

"The estate, of course," the duke replied, as though Benjamin was a simpleton. "I have a few estates to my name, as you know, but one of the smaller ones is not as profitable as I would like. I had been meaning to go there and inspect it myself, but now I think it might be the right place for you."

Benjamin blinked rapidly, relief that he was not about to be thrown out from the family circle flooding him.

"The estate is some distance away, however, and I do not expect you to return to town within the year. However, should you give up and leave in order to chase your pleasures once more, then I shall have no choice but to cut you from my will."

Benjamin pressed his lips together, trepidation filling him. "But Father, I have no experience. How am I to know how to manage anything?"

"I hired the finest tutors for you and sent you to Eton, did I not? The rest you shall have to learn," came the brisk reply. "You have been idle for too long, Benjamin. You need some kind of endeavor to allow you to focus on what you want your life to be, for I assure you that you cannot spend it indulging yourself – as I hope you have already begun to see."

Benjamin gave a swift nod, knowing that he could not refuse to do as his father asked, despite feeling as though he was about to leap into the unknown. To leave his friends behind and to go to an entirely new situation was quite a thought, despair beginning to fill him. "What if I fail, Father?" he asked, quietly. "What if I cannot make the estate any more profitable than it already is?"

There was a long pause, as the duke considered the question. Benjamin bit his lip, waiting for his father's judgement to fall.

"In one year, I shall look at your progress," came the eventual reply. "I have already written to my steward there. He will be awaiting you. He shall write reports to me regarding the estate and how you are managing things. Do not expect him to do everything for you, however, Benjamin. He is there to teach you should you request it of him, but many things you shall simply have to take the time to learn. If, after one year, the estate has not improved, I shall look over the reports and, if I am satisfied that you have done your utmost, then that shall be all there is to the matter."

"And if it is clear I have not?"

His father chuckled, but there was little humour within it. "Should you choose to continue with your laziness and sloth, leaving your steward to handle matters while you fall back into old habits, then I shall have to consider the consequences of such actions. It may or may not include an adjustment of my will, but that will be entirely determined by what you do."

An icy hand gripped Benjamin's heart, as he became aware that his father had done just as he intended and as his mother threatened. When his father spoke as such, there was weight behind the words. Benjamin was afraid, afraid that he could not work as hard as his father expected and, in doing so, put his entire future in jeopardy.

"I am quite sure you can do this, Benjamin," his father said, softly. "You are a good man, a better man that you have been acting as of late. A lack of direction has left you filling the void with untoward behavior. I believe this will ultimately be good for your character. Trust me when I say that I have no desire for you to be without your inheritance. I only do this in order to assist you."

Benjamin managed a tight smile. "I am aware of that, Father. Last night made a few things clear to me."

"Then I have every hope that you will succeed," his father said, gravely, rising from his chair. "We will miss seeing you here, Benjamin, but you will need to remain at that estate if you are to make a good go of it. Perhaps the allure of some of the more feminine kind will become less appealing by the time you return. Mayhap you might even consider matrimony!"

A quiet chuckle rumbled in his father's chest as he shook Benjamin's hand. "Be sure to write to us, to let us know how you fare. Your mother loves you as much as I do and I know she would be dreadfully upset not to hear from you."

Benjamin shook his head. "I believe Mama will be glad to see the back of me," he said, miserably, "after all that I have put her through."

His father's face softened. "However you feel about your mother, she acts as she does because she cares for you and wants only what is best. You are her son and she will always love you, no matter how much you frustrate her. It is one of the trials that comes with being a parent."

Benjamin could find nothing to say in response.

"Now, on you go and get yourself organized," the duke said, leading him toward the door of the study. "I shall have the carriage brought around in an hour."

"An hour?" Benjamin stared at his father, thunderstruck. "I am to leave today? For an entire year?" He had thought that he would have been allowed a few days' grace to get used to the idea of leaving, have a few last nights of well-behaved fun with his friends as he organized his things, but apparently his father thought otherwise.

"The sooner you get there, the sooner you can begin!" his father exclaimed, slapping him on the back. "On you go now. Your new home awaits. Oh, and Benjamin?"

"Yes, Father?"

"Be respectable. Leave the maids and the townswomen alone," his father said with a tilt of his head that implied more than he said.

"I will," he promised, nodding to his father that he understood his meaning.

Benjamin made his way along the hallway, his steps slow and measured. This all seemed very well prepared. He got the distinct impression that his father had been planning this venture for some time, aware that at some point he was going to have to intervene in Benjamin's life.

"This will not be so bad," he told himself, ignoring the way his heart lurched at the thought of leaving. He had never been very good at being alone. "I can do this."

The truth was, Benjamin was nervous. He was about to leave town, leave his family and friends without a word and travel to some far off county without knowing what on earth he was meant to do, not to return for an entire year. At least the estate was not in decline, for that would have meant a far greater struggle.

"Benjamin?"

His mother emerged from the drawing room, and Benjamin was surprised to see her eyes sparkling with tears.

"Hello, Mama."

"He has told you, then?"

"I think it for the best, Mama," Benjamin replied, catching her hand. "If you knew what I did, you would be glad that I am gone from your house."

A look of concern passed across her face.

"I am sorry for how I have spoken to you of late," Benjamin continued, quietly. "I do hope that I can do what Father asks."

"I am quite sure you can," his mother replied, with a fervency that astonished him. Apparently, he was not as little in his mother's estimation as he had thought.

"Is the carriage going soon?"

"Within the hour," Benjamin replied, with a quick smile. "Apparently Father wants me gone from London as soon as possible – which I, unfortunately, cannot protest against."

His mother nodded, and he bent to kiss her cheek before dropping her hand, turning on his heel, and walking away from the life he knew.

CHAPTER 6

*S*ophie held her breath as she stepped out of her bedchamber, clinging to the shadows. Mrs. Andrews had taken her bag down the stairs already, knowing that the master would not pay her any attention, given that he was still focused on Sophie. She hadn't heard from him for a few hours and, since then, Sophie had grown more and more nervous.

It was not as if she did not want to escape, but her worry was about leaving the house. If Malcolm caught her, dressed in her warmest clothes with her cloak and bonnet, then he'd know at once what she was doing. On top of that, heading out to an unknown estate, following the directions Mrs. Andrews had given her, was quite intimidating. She had no choice, however. It was either stay here and be forced against her will or leave and start an entirely new life.

It was a life in which she had no experience however, although Sophie knew she would give everything she had to it. As the daughter of a viscount, cleaning, scrubbing, and cooking were not exactly everyday activities. Sophie, however, was more than willing to learn. Besides which, the cook, maids, housekeeper, and other staff of this estate were the kindest people she had ever had the chance to come across. They had been her only friends in what had been very lonely months.

Softly padding down the staircase, moving as slowly as possible, Sophie paused as a sound caught her ears. She didn't know where it had come from. Everything in her wanted to run, headlong, down the stairs and then down the servant's staircase, but to do so would be utter foolishness. Panic swirled in her heart as she continued to wait, her fingers tightening on the bannister.

The sound came again – and this time, Sophie recognized it for what it was. A snore. Malcolm was snoring but, to her surprise, the sound was coming from down the stairs and not from his bedchamber.

The house was eerily dark, with only the moonlight streaming through the windows as Sophie's guide. Continuing down the staircase, she heard the snore again and realized, to her horror, that he was lying across the bottom step.

His head lolled ungainly against the stair, one arm draped across it, while the rest of him lay on the floor. His mouth was wide open, with the snores and occasional grunts emanating from it, his eyes completely closed. That did not mean, however, that Sophie was relieved at the sight of him. Instead, terror hit her hard, her breath catching. She was going to have to step very close to him, if not over him, if she was to get past.

What if he was just pretending to be asleep? What if this was his way of trying to capture her? Her mind worked furiously as her body refused to move, her eyes staring down at Malcolm's prone form.

Come on, Sophie, she told herself firmly, trying to bolster her courage. *Just a few more steps and you can be free.*

Forcing herself to move forward, she carefully moved

closer to him, wincing as the stairs creaked beneath her feet. He didn't even stir, the sound of his snores filling the hallway.

"Come now, miss!"

Startled, Sophie looked up, only to see one of the maids standing in her night things, holding out her hand toward Sophie. In the other hand, she held a single candle. The flickering light brought a reassurance to Sophie's quailing heart, her flagging spirit slowly heartening.

"He's been asleep for an hour after the drink took him under — you won't wake him," the maid promised, her whispers carrying across the room to Sophie. "Now hurry!"

With a deep breath, Sophie carefully placed her feet down beside her cousin, feeling his breath catch her ankles. With a shudder, she moved down the last two stairs and away from him, lifting her skirts high. She kept waiting for his ungodly roar to reach her ears, for his strong hands to grasp at her shoulder, but nothing happened. The room was just as still as before, his snores still regular and uninterrupted. Without a backward glance, Sophie hurried forward and clasped the maid's hand. The girl led her down the back staircase toward the servants' entrance. Mrs. Andrews was waiting for her, as was the housekeeper, Mrs. Smith.

"I don't want any of you to be in danger from him," Sophie whispered, as Mrs. Andrews enveloped her in a warm hug. "What if he blames you?"

"He won't," Mrs. Smith replied, calmly. "He's a proud and arrogant man, who thinks he knows better than anyone else. I promise that he won't consider for a moment that we've worked together to help you. We'll all vouch for one another and say we've been sound asleep and that you must have done it yourself."

Sophie tried to smile, but could only nod. "I can't thank you all enough."

"We'd never have left you here with him," the cook replied, firmly. "He's a menace and the way he's been treating you is sickening. The sooner we can all find better positions, the happier I'll be!"

Stepping outside into the cold night air, Sophie wondered if that would ever really be the case. Servants could very rarely find a new position without a reference which meant that, most likely, Malcolm's staff were stuck here. She was more grateful to them than she could say, and felt guilty she would be taking a position herself, due to the kindness of women here and at the new estate.

"I'll do what I can to help you leave here," she promised, as the groomsman helped her up onto her horse – one of the only things Malcolm had allowed her to take from her home. "I won't ever forget you."

The assembled servants didn't say another word, too afraid that their voices might carry. Instead, they waved and Sophie, pressing her hand to her heart, drank in the sight of those who had helped her. Urging the horse forward, she made her way out of the gate. Without looking back.

* * *

THE JOURNEY WAS MISERABLE. It was cold and damp, and Sophie felt as though her very bones were beginning to freeze. She made every attempt to follow the directions Mrs. Andrews had given her, having only the light of the moon to show her the path. With every minute that passed, Sophie was quite sure that Malcolm would be following her, riding up behind her and grabbing the horse's bridle. Then he would demand to know where she had been intending to go and would punish her for leaving. The fear clutching at her heart was so overwhelming that it exhausted her.

"He will no longer touch me," she whispered, as the cold

wind wrapped itself around her, finding the holes in her coat and pushing inside. Sophie shivered violently, her eyes squinting into the darkness at a single light glowing in the distance.

Was this the inn the cook had told her about? She had to hope it was. Patting her pocket, she felt the coins hidden inside, praying they would be enough to for a room as well as, hopefully, some food. The groom had instructed her to sell her horse so that it could not be found by Malcolm, and, although her heart squeezed at the thought of selling her beloved mare, Sophie knew she had no choice. She had thrown a shoe not far back and Sophie would be unable to pay a groom for the repair.

"Come on, old girl," she murmured, patting the horse's flanks. "Just a little bit longer and then we shall be quite safe."

She was nearing the entrance when she saw a carriage pull up to the front of the inn. It was a fine carriage, one that spoke of wealth and nobility. Sophie hung back in the shadows as she saw a man step forward out of the carriage. He was tall, and the light of the wall sconce caught the fine features of his face, his dark hair flowing away from his forehead. Sophie took in the breadth of his shoulders and the muscle under his tight-fitting pantaloons, before scolding herself for her prying eyes from the shadows.

What was such a man doing at an inn in the middle of the country? Did he know her cousin? She was certain she had never seen him before, but then, she had only been with Malcolm six months and had remained in the country all that time.

She went round the back to the stables, giving the reins of her mare to the groom who greeted her.

"Hello, Miss," he said, "is this the only horse?"

He looked around as if expecting her to have a companion with her.

"Yes," she replied, not providing additional information.

"Very good then," he said, a wide smile on his lips. "My apologies if no one was available to help you. The owner was not expecting the additional company this evening and is all in a flutter. A son of the Duke of Ware arrived unexpectedly."

"I see," she said, the name ringing round her head. He must be the son of the owner of the estate where she was headed. She had not believed any of the family to be in residence, which was part of the draw of the posting. She did not want to have left Malcolm only to find herself fending off the attentions of another just like him. Perhaps, however, she was mistaken and he would be kind.

At any rate, she knew right now more than anything she needed sleep. She entered the inn, relieved to find the main entry way empty but for the wife of the innkeeper. She led Sophie to a room without event, where Sophie fell into a deep sleep for the first time in many nights.

CHAPTER 7

*B*enjamin pushed himself up from the uncomfortable bed, rubbed his eyes, and sighed. The inn did not have the most welcoming of rooms, but, thankfully, this was his last stop before he arrived at his new estate. He did not know what to expect, but he would be glad to sleep in a proper bed at least.

Rising, he dressed himself quickly without his valet, sucking in a breath as the cold air hit his bare flesh. Stamping his feet to get some warmth back into his toes, he realized as he did that this was the earliest he had woken in some time.

He opened the door to his room, his eyes still half closed as he emerged into the hallway.

"Oof!" Something — make that some*one* — collided into his chest, causing him to take a step backward into the doorframe as he reached out reflexively.

"Bloody he…" his curse died out as he looked down at the person he now held in his arms, having caught her before she fell, and was rendered speechless by the face staring into his. Light freckles dusted a pert nose, atop rosy pink lips and high cheekbones. The only flaw seemed to be slightly crooked bottom front teeth, yet somehow they added to the drawing allure of her face.

The eyes staring up at him were close enough that he could see the gold flecks in them as they widened, so startled was she. She seemed to have been coming from the room next to his and must have been moving at quite the pace to have run into him so hard.

She was just a slip of a thing, but he stood riveted to the spot, mesmerized by her.

"Pardon me," she said stepping back from his arms, and after a moment of hesitation she was off, leaving him staring after her.

Behave, he told himself. He had not yet even reached his estate and already he was quite taken with the first beautiful woman who had, quite literally, stepped into his path. He shook his head and walked from the room in search of some sustenance.

"My lord!"

Benjamin grimaced at the innkeeper's cheery welcome, not feeling half as awake as he appeared to be. "Good morning."

"I'll bring you something to eat in just a moment, my lord," the man continued, indicating a rough-hewn wooden table with a jug of water and something that looked like coffee already sitting on it. "Please, have a seat."

Muttering his thanks, Benjamin sat down, eyeing the cup suspiciously. It looked more like sludge than coffee, although he could not help but enjoy the aroma that rose from it. Lifting it to his lips, he took a tentative sip – and was quite surprised to find it was not as bad as he had thought. He looked up as his coachman approached.

"Milord, begging your pardon for interrupting you when you are to be having breakfast, but there's a woman here who says she's headed to your estate."

Mildly irritated at being disturbed, Benjamin looked up at him. "And what of it?"

"She was asking if she might sit with me on the box, milord. She has a horse, but it has thrown a shoe and she has not the money to have it repaired."

"And what is this lady to be doing at my estate?" Benjamin asked, taking another sip of his coffee.

"Of the maids, I believe."

Benjamin shrugged. "Very well. Let her sit up top."

"And what of the horse? She said she means to sell it, but there's no time if we are to leave shortly."

Rolling his eyes, Benjamin shook his head. "Tell them to send me the bill for the shoe and bring the beast with us." What a maid was doing with a horse, he could not understand, but, wanting to be left in peace, he dismissed the coachman and waited for his breakfast.

* * *

AFTER HE BROKE HIS FAST, Benjamin readied himself for the short trip to his estate. He made his way to his carriage, having forgotten the passenger that was to accompany him until he saw two figures sitting atop. Before climbing in, he glanced up, only to find himself staring into eyes that were all too familiar — ones he had seen scarcely an hour earlier. This time Benjamin saw more in her expression. Within the biggest brown eyes Benjamin had ever seen, he also saw a large amount of fear.

For a reason Benjamin could not explain, he simply could not draw his gaze away from her and she, despite her station, continued to look at him. Managing to clear his throat, and reminding himself firmly that she was a servant and nothing more, Benjamin managed a small smile. "So we meet again. You are the new maid, are you?"

"I am," she replied, before dropping her gaze. "I mean, I am, my lord." A sudden flush covered her cheeks and Benjamin thought that she was one of the most exquisite creatures he'd ever had the chance to see. Struck by just how inappropriate such a thought was, Benjamin tugged his eyes away from the lady and went to sit inside, wondering as he did at her ability to afford such a room at the inn.

As the carriage moved away, however, Benjamin's thoughts turned and he berated himself for allowing his mind to become so tainted by a pair of beautiful eyes such as the lady had. He was here to become a new man, was he not? And that meant that he would treat his staff with respect and consideration, and *not* have his way with any of the maids. That would be particularly difficult when such a fine specimen was among them, but Benjamin was determined to show his father that he was a changed man.

* * *

"Here we are, milord!"

The cheerful shout of the coachman had Benjamin start in surprise, and he realized he'd fallen asleep. Were they here? Looking out of the window, Benjamin saw the rather large white stucco house coming into view. In front were small gardens, but what seemed to be an extensive forest spread beyond the back of the estate. The gardens, while maintained, looked as though they could do with a fresh start, particularly since they lacked any amount of color. The house itself appeared to be in decent condition, although some of the statues out front had the first touches of green. He would have to ensure the gardener got rid of any kind of moss or lichen for he thought the estate should have a somewhat grand appearance.

The carriage stopped just outside the front door and

Benjamin was pleased to find the staff all lined up to meet him. He descended the carriage steps to be first greeted by the only two he remembered from his previous visits — the butler, Smithers, and the housekeeper, Mrs. Martins. They introduced him to the rest and he nodded to each staff member, in turn.

"I am very glad to be here," he said jovially to the assembled staff. "I am sure we shall all get along splendidly." He dismissed them and, turning back to the housekeeper, indicated the maid who was climbing down from the carriage.

"This is our new maid," he said, missing the startled expression on Mrs. Martins' face. "The coachman met her at the inn. Something about a horse throwing a shoe, which is why she came with me. The horse itself can be stabled for the time being. At length, I shall talk to her about the creature and what we are to do with it."

"Of course, my lord," the housekeeper murmured, her eyes on the new maid. "It is very good of you to bring her here."

"Well," Benjamin chuckled, "I could not exactly leave her at the inn now, could I? Although why we need another maid, I am not quite sure, given that there appears to be so many staff members already!"

The housekeeper's eyes flashed. "We certainly do need her, My Lord. The house is large and there are a great many duties."

He shrugged, surprised at how strongly the woman had responded. "You know the household best, Mrs. Martins. I defer to your better judgement."

The maid, by this time, was standing just to his left, her eyes fixed on the ground. She was smaller and slighter than his original judgment. He hoped that she was not about to faint, given how pale she looked. Perhaps she had travelled a long distance and was merely exhausted.

"No duties for her today, Mrs. Martins," he said, wondering what had brought these words to his lips. He should not be showing special attention to any of the staff. "Ensure she is fed too, for she looks about to faint." He smiled at the astonished housekeeper, confusion swirling in his chest as to why he had been so concerned over one of his servants.

"You are very kind, my lord," came the maid's low voice, but Benjamin merely shrugged.

"I had best go inside now and explore my new home," he said, with a smile. "Mrs. Martins, a tray in the study, if you please. Coffee, not tea."

"At once, my lord," Mrs. Martins replied, bobbing a curtsy. Benjamin nodded, giving one last look up at the house before walking inside.

* * *

THE HOUSE WAS large but not overly so. Benjamin wandered through it at his leisure, seeing it with new eyes as his responsibility, before eventually finding his way back to the study. The tea tray was sitting on his father's broad mahogany pedestal desk, which gave Benjamin an uncomfortable feeling as he went to sit behind it. There was something about being at this side of the desk, as opposed to being sat in front of it. A sense of duty, of purpose.

"Although I am not sure whether I can fulfil those requirements," Benjamin muttered to himself, adding a little milk to his coffee. He could not pretend that he was not already missing the pleasures of town, for they had been such a big part of his life for so long that to be without left something of a hole within him. To go from a large group of friends to none whatsoever felt strange. A sense of loneliness wrapped itself around Benjamin's heart, and he sank back into his chair with a sigh.

"Perhaps I ought to send for a couple of friends," he muttered to himself, his lips twisting into a grimace. He had no doubt what his father would say if he heard that Benjamin had recalled his friends from town. Then again, it was not up to the old man what Benjamin did and who he had to stay.

But I want to succeed, Benjamin thought to himself. The truth was, if he did choose to invite his friends, then chances were that he would, more than likely, be drawn back into that way of living. He would ultimately fail, his estate would fall, and he would be cut from his father's will. No, he could not ask his friends from town.

"Although I might ask some I have not seen for some time," he mused to himself, pulling open the desk drawers to his right and left one at a time until he found some parchment. Twirling the quill pen that had been resting on the leather desktop between his hands for a moment, Benjamin dipped it in the inkwell and began the first of two letters, requesting the pleasure of each man's company at his new estate. He had not seen either fellow for a good few years, but now seemed like as good a time as any to re-establish their acquaintance. They both lived nearby, were unmarried, and owned their own title and estate, so Benjamin reasoned that they might be of some assistance to him, given that he had very little idea of what to do.

His quill scratched over the paper for a few minutes more until both letters were sanded, folded and sealed. Then, getting to his feet, Benjamin rang the bell and stood by the window, looking out over the gardens of his estate. His heart swelled with a sudden pride as he drew in a deep breath, master — for the time being — of all that he surveyed.

"Yes, my lord?"

"I have two letters here," Benjamin replied, holding them

up. "And might you send up some of the accounts? I suppose I should look over them."

The butler took the two letters but did not retreat. Instead, he set them down, walked to the other end of the study and opened a large drawer in the bookcase cabinet.

"You will find all the accounts here, my lord," he said, setting down a large book on Benjamin's desk. "The steward is available to see you and speak with you whenever you wish."

"Make an appointment with him for tomorrow," Benjamin replied, sitting down again and running his fingers over the book's worn cover. "Say two o'clock in the afternoon."

The butler nodded and picked up Benjamin's letters. "Of course, my lord. Can I get you anything else?"

Benjamin shook his head, pulling open the front cover of the book and finding that it was filled with nothing but numbers.

"There is fresh brandy in the decanter, my lord," the butler continued, when Benjamin did not reply. "And dinner will be served very soon."

Benjamin muttered something unintelligible and waved the butler away, entirely taken up with the accounts book. Running his finger down the length of one page, he looked at all the numbers and the small description next to each one of what had been purchased.

The problem was that Benjamin was not particularly good with numbers. He could already feel his head beginning to thump as he tried his best to work out what had been coming in and what had been going out. While everything appeared to be in order, if he did not go through the accounts himself, how could he be sure that there were no discrepancies? He had to make sure that he knew the intricacies of what went on at his estate, and that meant getting his head around the figures.

He bit back a sigh as his mental arithmetic failed him, yet again. With a quiet groan, he put his head in his hands. A sharp longing for London and all the pleasures that came with it pierced him, but Benjamin batted it away. He could not lose himself in daydreams about returning to that life, or get mired down in self-pity. He *had* to do this. He had to succeed, for to return a failure meant that his future would be very different from what he had planned. There would be time for frivolity and joviality at a later date, but at this present moment, he had to embrace his new responsibilities and tasks with a fierce determination that, currently, he did not feel.

"Perhaps I shall look at the accounts tomorrow," he muttered to himself, closing the book and pushing it to one side. Seeing the brandy decanter in the corner, Benjamin rose and poured himself a measure into a glass, swirling it around before taking a sip.

"I can do this," he told himself, repeatedly, as the brandy slowly built a fire in his limbs. "I will not fail."

CHAPTER 8

"*I* am so very grateful to you all," Sophie said, grasping the cook's warm hands. "I did not know what would become of me."

The cook, Mrs. Potts, smiled, her blue eyes twinkling. "I am very glad to have you here, Madam. It's not every day we have a lady become part of the serving staff. I must confess, it's quite unorthodox!"

"But necessary, " Mrs. Martins interjected. "When I heard of your plight, and how very alone you were, I could not have ignored such news. However, that was before we knew Lord Benjamin was coming."

Sophie felt her cheeks burn. "He seems a very kind man, to be sure," she murmured quietly.

"Kind?" Mrs. Potts chuckled, shaking her head. "I'm not sure kind is an accurate description of him. The boy — while man, now — has been wrapped up in himself since the day he was born." She made to say more but, with a disapproving look from the housekeeper, she murmured, "I suppose he's not the worst sort, though. He certainly won't cause you any danger as you were in before," before lapsing into silence.

"Regardless, I am grateful that he was willing to drive me here," Sophie replied, with a lift of one shoulder.

Mrs. Martins gave her a tight smile. "I am quite sure you will get to know his true nature very soon. He has been here on previous occasions, although that was many years ago. However, two of the footmen were sent here from the London townhouse. They have brought a great many tales with them which, of course, I have discouraged from being spread around the house, but it seems it cannot be helped."

Sophie tried to smile and nod but ended up feeling a little sick. She had found Lord Harrington both a handsome and considerate gentleman, but that had only been on the briefest of acquaintances. She might well be wrong. It had taken her some time to determine Malcolm's true nature. Was she truly such a terrible judge of character?

"Now," Mrs. Martins continued, leading her into the housekeeper's small private parlor, where a tea tray sat waiting for them. "I know that the situation you are in does not place you where you ought to be, but I believe you wish to hide from your cousin for a time."

"Yes," Sophie breathed, a frisson of fear racing down her back as the housekeeper handed her a cup of tea. "My cousin has been quite intent on pressing his intentions on me, and while I was always able to hide in my room, the staff told me that he planned to remove the lock and replace it with a new one so that he might have the key." Her tea sloshed over the side of her cup when she shuddered. "I hate to impose, but I have nowhere else to turn."

Mrs. Martins nodded slowly, her lined face grim. "Yes, I was told that you had no other family to speak of."

"None," Sophie admitted, trying to keep the sadness from her face. "When my parents died, I was sent to live with Malcolm, who is my distant cousin. I have no one else in the world who might care for me."

Carefully topping up Sophie's teacup, Mrs. Martins looked up at Sophie thoughtfully. "Then I am glad to have you here, even though it is a very unusual situation. You are quite sure you are willing to take on the role of a servant?" Her expression betrayed a difficulty in believing that Sophie would be capable of doing such a thing.

"I will do whatever I have to," Sophie answered, firmly. "I cannot go back to my cousin, and I must have food and shelter if I am to survive. I know Malcolm will look for me, and if I am found, then I know not what he shall do."

The housekeeper did not look in the least bit perturbed. "I am quite sure he will not look for you among the staff," she said, firmly. "That is why I agreed to Mrs. Potts' suggestion. It is only she and I that know of your true identity, so be prepared to be treated by the rest of the staff as another maid."

Sophie managed a slight smile. "I should be glad to be thought of as one of them," she replied, at once. "I do not want to be treated any differently, although I do not have any experience in cleaning and dusting." Heat hit her cheeks as she realized just how foolish she sounded. "I mean, I have other skills such as arithmetic and geography, but I hardly think they will be particularly useful at the moment!"

"Unfortunately not," Mrs. Martins commented, with a slightly rueful smile. "However, we will do what we can. You might prove more useful to assist me with my duties, given that arithmetic and the like are more often a part of my responsibilities than the maids."

Sophie managed a soft laugh, desperately wondering if she would manage to do what was required of her. Doubts began to plague her as Mrs. Martins rose from her chair, ready to show Sophie her room. Sophie followed, bag in hand, hearing the housekeeper say something about a uniform. She was given a few curious glances by the other servants, who, by this time, were gathering together for their own luncheon. Sophie tried to smile at each one that passed her but was given no words of welcome. She hoped the icy reception was not an indication of what was to come.

"Here," Mrs. Martins smiled, opening the door into what was the smallest room Sophie had ever seen. "I am quite sure this is not the size you are used to but it is, at least, private and you can lock it from the inside. No one will bother you, but the key to the lock is already in the door."

Sophie smiled and thanked her, appreciating her kindness.

"Do come through to eat with the rest of us," Mrs. Martins replied, making to close the door. "Once you are settled in, of course."

Promising that she would, Sophie stood by the bed and looked around the small room. It was almost the same size as her previous dressing room had been, long and narrow. There was a bed in one corner, a small table and a few candles. That was all. There was no fire but plenty of blankets. Sophie could not imagine what it would be like to dress in the morning, wondering whether there would be ice on the inside of the small, narrow window. She shivered at the thought, placing her bag on the bed. The frame creaked as she sat down next to it, making her wonder whether or not it would truly take her weight.

But Sophie determined that she would not complain. Yes, the room was nothing like she was used to and certainly a lot smaller, but it was better than remaining in her large room at Malcolm's estate with the sound of his determined bellow ringing in her ears. And, at least here she felt safe, even though she was taking on a role that was not hers and certainly did not belong to her. She had no idea how to cook or clean, and was certain she would look like a most incompetent maid. The last thing she needed was for the master to consider her a very strange thing and get rid of her – for she needed both the job and the security.

"Then I shall just put my mind to it and learn," she muttered to herself and, getting to her feet, began to take things from her bag and set them about the room. Her clothes neatly away, Sophie pulled out the last of her items – a small miniature of her parents. She gazed at it for a moment, her heart squeezing painfully. If only they had lived, how different life would have been.

Brushing away a single tear, Sophie set her shoulders and determined to make the best of the situation. She could do this. She *would* to do this. She had no other choice.

* * *

"Now," Mrs. Martins murmured, as she helped Sophie tie up her hair following the mid-day meal, "we shall go and introduce you to the master and I will ask him specifically if I can train you. I shall say some such thing about you having more skills than I first realized, and that I think you could do with some additional training and that you might be a help to me." She gave Sophie a kind smile. "I think that would do you better than dusting and the like."

Sophie did not quite manage to curve her lips, tension rolling around in her stomach at the thought of meeting Lord Harrington again. He was handsome, to be sure, but when the cook had described him, he sounded much like Malcolm. She had hoped to try to escape his notice as best she could.

"Remember not to look directly at him, and curtsy when you first go in," the housekeeper continued, as she began to walk briskly toward the servant's stairs. "I shall do most of the talking, although be prepared to answer any questions he might have."

"Yes, of course," Sophie mumbled, her heart all in a flutter. She resisted the urge to straighten her dress – a long, high-necked, dark creation that certainly added to her attempts to look like a servant, and followed in behind Mrs. Martins.

"Ah, good evening, Mrs. Martins," Lord Harrington mumbled, not looking at either of them as he continued to stare into the bright orange and red flames that licked up the wood and coal in the grate, his wrist turning as he swirled the drink in his hand. "The butler mentioned that you wanted to discuss something with me."

"I thank you for your time, my lord," Mrs. Martins replied at once, with a slight bow of her head. "What I wanted to speak to you about was our new maid."

Lord Harrington glanced over at them both, his brows rising to see Sophie standing there who realized, too late, that she had been much too busy studying Lord Harrington. His dark hair hung over his brow, his shirt open at the neck, naked without a cravat in the privacy of his home. She could see tufts of hair rising above it. With sculpted cheekbones, an aquiline nose, and dark blue eyes that seemed to see right through her, his appearance caused heat to flood in her belly.

"The new maid who is present at this very moment?" Lord Harrington murmured, his gaze raking over her from head to toe.

"Indeed," Mrs. Martins answered, as Sophie dropped her eyes to the floor, her cheeks burning from being caught staring. "She has proven herself to have skills that would be of an assistance to me. I would ask, therefore, that she be allowed to help me in my work. Perhaps I might even train her."

"So she can go off and find herself another place of employment?" Lord Harrington chuckled, shaking his head. "Goodness, Mrs. Martins! I do hope you are not trying to take my servants away from me before they've even started."

"No, of course I am not, my lord," Mrs. Martins replied,

sounding more than a little flustered. "I simply meant that she would, at least, be a good addition to your household should she be allowed to use the skills she has."

"And what skills are these?" Lord Harrington asked, his eyes now back on Sophie, who glanced up at Mrs. Martins. She saw Mrs. Martins give the tiniest of nods, telling her that she should respond to Lord Harrington herself.

"I can do arithmetic," she stammered, not quite sure what else to say. "I can read and write very well."

"Is that so?" Lord Harrington murmured, suddenly throwing himself from his chair and coming to stand in front of her. "And how is it that a maid comes to have such skills as these?"

Sophie's mouth went dry. She did not raise her head but was more than aware of him standing in front of her. His presence filled the room, seemingly surrounding her on every side.

"I believe she assisted the governess in a previous charge," Mrs. Martins said, hastily, when Sophie remained mute. "Obviously, when the children grew, there was no need for her anymore."

There was a long silence. Sophie did not know what to say or what to do, standing frozen on the spot. Lord Harrington remained in front of her, as though stuck to the floor. Sophie felt her breath catch in her chest as one long finger reached out and lifted her chin until she was forced to look directly into his face.

"You are very young to have been with a governess until the children flew the nest," he commented, frowning.

Sophie swallowed the sudden lump of fear in her throat and tried to smile. "The children left for Eton at seven years old and there was but two of them," she stammered, relieved that she had come up with a reasonable explanation. "Both boys, of course."

His eyes caught hers and refused to let her look away. The intensity of his gaze sparked both terror and warmth in her heart, swirling them together until she was utterly confused. She could only hope that he would accept what she said, for she could not come up with any other kind of explanation.

After what seemed like an eternity, he dropped her chin and stepped back, seemingly satisfied.

"I suppose you might help Mrs. Martins, then," he said, glancing over at the housekeeper. "Although we will not have difficulties with the rest of the maids, then, I hope?"

"No, not in the least," Mrs. Martins promised. "I can assure you that there are enough of them to fulfil all that is expected and more."

Sophie closed her eyes briefly in relief, feeling her shoulders slump as the tension in her body drained away. She felt a slight touch on her arm and, seeing Mrs. Martins nodding toward the door, began to hurry toward it, suddenly desperate to remove herself from Lord Harrington's presence. He disconcerted her, although she couldn't quite say why.

"However," came his strong voice. "At times, I may require your assistance. Should your arithmetic and writing skills be up to scratch, then I have a lot of paperwork you may help me go through."

Mrs. Martins grasped Sophie's arm and turned her back around to face the master.

"But of course," Mrs. Martins replied as Sophie pasted a smile on her face. "I am quite sure she would be delighted to help you."

"And what do I call you?" Lord Harrington asked, directing the question at Sophie. "I confess that I remember very few of the names of my staff, but I believe that you are to be the exception in this case."

Sophie stared at him, the words of introduction dying on

her lips. She had not thought of another name for herself, and certainly could not give him her own name.

"This is Sarah, my lord," Mrs. Martins said, quickly. "I am sorry, she is something of a mouse."

His lips quirked. "A mouse, are you? Very quiet indeed." He watched her for a moment longer before turning on his heel and shrugging. "Very good. I shall call for you tomorrow, Sarah. I must see how good these so-called 'skills' of yours really are before I will know for certain whether you are to be of any use to me."

CHAPTER 9

*B*enjamin was not feeling his best when he rose the following morning. He had drunk a little too much fine brandy the previous evening without even realizing it and now as a consequence had a painful headache to accompany it.

However, the breakfast tray arrived with, pleasantly, two letters. Both were from his friends, both accepting his invitation to stay with him for a short time. That, at least, brought a smile to his face. He was already beginning to find this place dull and he had only just arrived.

As he ate his toast, Benjamin tried not to think of the pretty maid who had invaded his home and his thoughts only yesterday. He was determined to prove to his father that he was able to run the estate well, but he was finding it difficult to shed his old habits. He could think of nothing but that the quiet little maid had one of the loveliest faces he had ever seen. Of course, her stark black dress somewhat hid the curves of her small frame, but he was quite sure there was a delectable figure beneath it.

However, Benjamin knew he could not act on such

thoughts. It would not only be morally reprehensible, but it could endanger Sarah's future. Of course, masters had taken their maids to bed for generations, but such a thing was only a consideration for their own pleasures and certainly not that of their servants. On top of which, Benjamin did not want anything to distract him from what he had to do – which was to ensure the estate brought in a profit and show his father that he could change his ways. He was determined to succeed.

Pushing himself out of bed, Benjamin rose and dressed, choosing not to call for Peter, his valet. A shirt and breeches would do quite nicely, given that he was to spend most of his day in the study going over the accounts. His steward would be with him in the afternoon, but he wanted to have a clear idea of the finances before that time came.

The third cup of coffee finally cleared his head and Benjamin strode toward the study, glad to see a fire in the grate already. The stack of accounts lay on his desk, exactly where he had left them, and Benjamin rounded the mahogany desk to sit in the wide leather chair to open them.

His eyes ran down the list of numbers, his fingers tracing over the page, one line after the other. Finding a piece of parchment, he grasped his quill pen and began scribbling down various calculations, wanting to ensure that everything was in order … but, before long, he became a touch confused.

Throwing down the pen, Benjamin sat back in exasperation. Arithmetic had never been something he had been particularly good at. It was as though there was something in his brain that simply did not want to process such things. Once the calculations became more difficult, his mind simply stopped working. It would chew over the numbers for a time, before spitting them out completely. Benjamin slumped back into his chair, a wave of embarrassment washing over him. He would not be any good to the steward with his lack of understanding of the ledgers.

Sighing, he rose and rang the bell. Perhaps it was time to see just how much this maid would be of benefit. It would be too embarrassing to ask for aid from another man, but a female would do quite nicely. Besides, as she was part of his staff, he could ensure she said not a word to anyone about what her duties were. That was only if she was able to help him, of course. The chances were she had over-exaggerated her talents in order to keep herself from dusting and cleaning like the other maids.

"Send up that new maid," he instructed the butler, the moment the scratch at the door was heard. "What was her name again? Sonia?"

"Sarah, My Lord," the butler intoned, with only a flicker of surprise. "You wish to see her?"

"At once," Benjamin instructed, with a wave of his hand. "And another tea tray if you please. I did not eat a lot of breakfast."

The butler nodded and left, closing the door firmly behind him. Benjamin rose to his feet and walked to the window behind the desk, leaning his forehead against the cool glass overlooking the brown gardens below. He was lonely, frustrated, and tired of this life of responsibility already. However, Benjamin knew he could not return to London. The disgrace he had found himself in would haunt him should he return, and being cut from his father's will would mean a lifetime of living on other people's charity, if not having to find some kind of employment. He shuddered at the thought, pushing himself up to stand tall once more, closing his eyes and drawing in a deep breath.

"I must do this," he muttered to himself, trying to steel his resolve. "I have to."

The truth was, there was very little choice. Perhaps the

company of his two friends would bring some joy to this place, although he would not let them know just how difficult he was finding the accounts. Numbers were still a mystery to him and Benjamin was ashamed at just how truly terrible he was at such things. He had managed to get through Eton on charm and reliance on friends who were much better with them than he was.

A soft knock on the door drew his attention and he walked over to open it himself. There stood Sarah, her hands folded in front of her and her head slightly bowed, spots of color in her cheeks. She was either terrified or delighted with his singular attentions. Given the tension in her features when she walked in, Benjamin guessed the former and determined he would put her at ease. He could not help but admire her slender neck and neatly-coiled chestnut hair. Fleetingly, he wondered what she would look like with her hair around her shoulders, free of its pins.

Steady.

Remembering that he was not meant to be indulging himself with such thoughts – and certainly not with any actions – Benjamin walked around to his desk and indicated that she stand next to him. She did so at once, not raising her eyes to his as she had done the day before.

"Now," Benjamin cleared his throat and began, running his finger down the open page of the accounts. "I want you to prove your skills to me."

"Prove them to you, my kord?" she asked, surprise in her voice as she looked up at him. "What do you wish me to do?"

"Go through this page of accounts and show me whether everything is in order," he said, briskly, picking up the heavy book and handing it to her. "There is a small writing desk in the corner where you can work. It should have everything you need."

She blinked at him for a moment, as though astonished at

his request, but took the book from him to do as he asked. Benjamin grimaced, wondering whether the look on her face meant she was suddenly terrified about what was expected of her. Was she truly able to do as she said?

For around half an hour, Benjamin sat back in his chair and studied Sarah. She had surprised him by getting to work at once, her brow furrowing in concentration. Whatever she was scribbling on the parchment to her right was evidently giving her the answers she needed, for a look of satisfaction grew on her face as she neared the end of the page.

Benjamin lifted his brows in surprise when she came back to him, parchment in her hand. Her fingers were slightly stained with ink but there was a brightness in her features that caught his attention. The slight curve of her lips made him smile, and he arched one eyebrow as she approached.

"Might I dare to think you have been successful?"

"Very," she replied, putting the parchment on his desk in front of him. "Here, you see? Most things are in order, but there is a slight miscalculation near the bottom of the page." She leaned down, a little closer to him than before, and he caught the scent of lavender as she pointed out what she meant. "The calculations for the meat and the flour were out by a few pennies, but I have rectified it. It is a small mistake, of course, so not in the least bit worrisome."

Benjamin glanced up at her, his breath suddenly catching in his throat at her nearness. Her cheeks were dusted with pink, her eyes bright and focused. When he forced himself to look away, down at the parchment, he was surprised to see beautiful, flowing handwriting.

"My goodness," he murmured, bending down a little closer so that he might have a better look. "You are quite something, Sarah. Are you quite sure you were meant to be a maid?"

She blushed and looked away, standing tall once more. "I was well trained, and it was very kind of the governess and my employers to allow me to learn."

"Yes, very," Benjamin murmured, finding himself quite taken with the young woman, his interest becoming more than simply desire. "I think you shall prove very useful to me, Sarah. I'm afraid the housekeeper shall see very little of you."

Providing her with another task, Benjamin could not help but allow his gaze to linger on her a little longer as she walked over to the desk which matched his. She was one of the most intriguing women he had ever met and Benjamin was not quite sure what to make of the little maid.

An hour or so passed and Sarah continued to work studiously. After some time, Benjamin could not help but walk over toward her, watching her work. Her brow was furrowed in concentration, her lips pursed, but her gaze remained steady and fixed. She was working hard, to the point that she seemed entirely unaware of his presence.

Benjamin watched as she continued to work through her calculations, making swift marks on the paper, coming up with – from what he guessed – the correct answer. He wished that he could work things out as easily as she, frustrated with himself over his lack of understanding.

"Might I help you, my lord?"

She was looking up at him, a confused expression on her face.

"Am I doing something wrong?" she asked when he did not respond immediately.

The look on her face as she gazed up at him lessened his frustration of his own inabilities. "No, indeed, Sarah. I was simply watching you work." A wry smile tugged at the corner of his lips. "I only wished I could do these calculations as easily as you."

She blinked twice, an expression of surprise on her face.

Benjamin cursed himself under his breath for being so open with her, a mere servant, when he knew he should not have said a word. It was not for a master to demean himself in such a way, even if the servant in question had a pretty face and a kind smile.

"Never mind," he grated, turning on his heel and walking away from her. "It matters not. Continue with your work."

"I apologize if I have done something wrong," she replied, once more missing the 'my lord' from the end of her sentence. "I did not mean to upset you."

He twisted his head to look back at her, seeing the hesitation in her expression, the worry in her eyes. Striding back toward her, he stopped as he saw her suddenly shrink back, as though terrified he was about to strike her.

His lingering frustration evaporated in a moment. Benjamin was not that kind of man, nor did he want his staff to think that he would ever do such a thing. What had caused her to shirk from him? Did the other staff warn her away from him?

"I will never hurt you, Sarah," he said, a little more gently. "I am not that kind of master, and I hope that the rest of my staff do not think I would ever do that kind of thing."

"No, indeed," she whispered, her face pale and strained. "I apologize. It was just a reaction from my... previous employment."

Benjamin's jaw tightened as he thought of what could have happened to her in the past to cause such fright.

"What happened?" he demanded.

"It is of no consequence—"

"What happened, Sarah?"

"I had an... employer who attempted to take liberties," she said quietly. "He became angry and violent when I did not allow him to do so."

He tensed in unexpected anger at the unknown man who would try to hurt her.

"Did he ever…"

"No, my lord," she said, her head bowed. "I was fortunate to find employment here and left before anything occurred."

"Good," he said with a curt nod, alarmed at the level of emotion he felt at her words.

"Earlier I was frustrated, that is all," he muttered, passing a hand over his brow. "Numbers and calculations do not come to me as easily as they ought. Neither should I have explained such a thing to you." He stepped away, returning to his study desk. Why had he said such a thing to her? Why had he tried to explain himself to a maid?

Dropping his head, Benjamin tried to focus on the correspondence at his desk instead of the servant girl working in the corner of the room who now peered at him in confusion. He had to focus on what was important, not on any potential carnal pleasures. Especially after what she had just told him of her past. Sighing to himself, Benjamin picked up one of his letters and began to read.

CHAPTER 10

"*Y*ou've been working too hard!"

Sophie smiled and tried to hide her yawn behind the back of her hand as Mrs. Martins led her into her sitting room. "Not too hard at all. Truthfully, I am quite enjoying it."

Mrs. Martins frowned. "He does call for you often."

That was true. Sophie had been summoned to the master's study almost every day for the last five days, spending hours working on his accounts and even on some correspondence. It was as though she was becoming his own personal secretary.

Not that it bothered her. It kept her mind busy and certainly was better suited to her than cleaning the floors or learning how to wash clothes. Sometimes Lord Harrington sat with her, other times she was alone. Unfortunately, however, Sophie had heard a few whispers about her going around the servants' quarters, but she supposed that could not be helped.

"I have heard what some are saying of me," she began,

seeing Mrs. Martins' sympathetic face. "Is there anything I can do about that?"

Mrs. Martins sighed and shook her head. "No, not much, I'm afraid. I have tried to stamp out gossiping, but it continues to grow. As the master's staff, we are not afforded the same rights as you have been used to, as a lady. It does not matter, for example, whether or not you are with the master alone. You are a servant, therefore, you do what you are instructed. You have no reputation to speak of here, as his domestic, but the others will gossip, out of jealousy if nothing else." She lifted one shoulder, her lined face grave. "Besides which, it doesn't help matters that the master has something of a reputation himself."

A curl of alarm rose in Sophie's throat.

"That being said, he has not attempted anything with any of the staff thus far, and I hope he will continue on that path. Nor have I ever heard of him forcing his attentions," Mrs. Martins finished, patting her hand. "Now, you finish your cup of tea and then off to bed with you. It is late and I'm quite sure the master will require your services in the morning. I'd best go chase those young things to their beds."

Sophie chuckled, knowing exactly which maids Mrs. Martins was talking about. She smiled to herself as she watched Mrs. Martins leave the room with the door ajar. Pouring herself another small cup of tea, Sophie added a dash of milk and settled back in her chair. She knew the other servants questioned her preferred treatment by both Lord Harrington and Mrs. Martins, but she tried not to let it worry her.

She was no longer as afraid as she had been, and was enjoying her new life here, even with the long hours and early mornings. It was better than living in constant fear, caught in a web with no way of escape. The only problem on her hands was the unexpected pull of attraction she felt to Lord Harrington.

Sophie hated that she was beginning to look forward to spending time in his company. It was more than pleasure at being called away from dusting, and she was finding her feelings quite disconcerting. He was handsome, of course, but she continually got the impression that there was something underneath the layers of self-assurance and pride that he was trying desperately to hide. He had not spoken to her of it, but there was frustration in his eyes whenever he came over to check her progress. There was, of course, the time he had mentioned finding calculations and the like more difficult than she, but that was not something he needed to be embarrassed about.

Sighing, she lifted the cup to her mouth and sipped at the hearty brew. Mayhap he was ashamed that he needed her help in order to fully understand his accounts or to go over any mistakes she had found. Gentlemen could be so pride filled.

Sophie felt her cheeks warm as she recalled how he had stood so very close to her, his waist at her shoulder as he had come to stand behind her, looking at her work. The scent of pine and nutmeg had drifted toward her, making her senses reel for just a moment. When he had brought his hand forward to point out something she had written, his fingers had brushed her shoulder, and her body had burned with a sudden, unexpected fire.

It was not wise to have any kind of affection for one's employer.

Besides which, Sophie was not exactly telling him the truth about who she was and what she was doing in his home. If he knew she was a lady, would it make any difference in his behavior toward her? Given what the staff said about him – that he was a rake who took his pleasures anywhere he wanted – Sophie had to believe that it was safer for her to remain a servant in his eyes, since he had not gone near a single maid since his return a week ago.

And while her instincts told her he would not take what was not freely given, she was hesitant to believe as such, given her past experience with Malcolm.

"You are quite foolish, you know," she told herself, picking up the tea tray and walking to the kitchen to wash up the dishes. "More than foolish. Idiotic."

Giving herself quite a firm telling off, Sophie began to wash the tea cups, bidding Mrs. Martins good night as she passed her in the long narrow corridor. The servants' quarters were quiet and still, and Sophie found herself enjoying the silence. The kitchen was warm still, after all the cooking of the day, and Sophie chose to sit down at the large wooden table in the center of the room and simply listen to the quiet.

It brought her a peace that she had not often experienced in her last year. Resting her head on her arms, Sophie smiled softly to herself, thinking just how blessed she had been to escape such a torment as that of her cousin. Her gaze lingered on the candle on the table, watching the pale glow of the candlelight spread across the kitchen.

She would take this moment of peace — as one never knew what was to come next.

* * *

A SUDDEN THUMP had her jerking upright, and she realized that she had fallen asleep. Blinking furiously, Sophie saw that her candle was burning low and that a chill had begun to spread across her shoulders. Whatever had been that noise?

Slowly getting up from the table, Sophie picked up her candle and began to make her way soundlessly toward her own quarters. Perhaps it had been nothing more than a mouse in the cellar, although it would have had to have been a very large mouse to make such a thump as she had heard. The thought made her smile, relieving some of the tension she felt. Walking slowly, she heard the sound again, followed by a series of muttered curses.

There was someone in the pantry.

Sophie took a breath and stepped forward, lifting her chin and curling one hand into a fist, just in case she should need a weapon. A small light from within the pantry told her she was quite right to assume that someone was within and, before thinking of the possible danger, she pushed the door open wide.

Lord Harrington stared back at her, his eyes wide, hair tousled and shirt almost completely untucked, the top buttons open to reveal the slight dusting of hair on top of the muscles of his chest.

"Oh, my lord!" Sophie stammered, suddenly not knowing where to look as her cheeks burned with color. "Do forgive me, I thought…"

"I can't find the brandy."

Sophie looked back at him again, seeing the slight wildness in his eyes. He had clearly drunk a little too much, although why he might be looking for brandy, when there was a plentiful supply in almost every room of the house, Sophie could not say.

"I know there is certainly brandy in your study, my lord," she said, quietly, entirely at a loss as to how to remove him from the pantry. Should she call the housekeeper? Or the butler?

"Not anymoret," he replied, his eyes glazing over just a little.

"The library then, or the drawing room?" Sophie asked, wondering how he had managed to come down the stairs without breaking his neck given how he staggered. "Let us search elsewhere. You will find none here."

It was a bold idea, but Sophie knew she could not leave him in the pantry, otherwise the cook would have a fit come the morning. It was already in a little bit of a mess, and he had managed to stand on some of the vegetables for tomorrow's dinner. More were at risk if Sophie could not remove him as soon as possible.

"Can you show me?" Lord Harrington asked as he reached for her. "The brandy, I mean. Nothing else." A quiet chuckle escaped from his chest, making Sophie's cheeks burn.

"Yes, of course," she murmured, trying not to react when he slung one arm around her waist, the emotions of desire and unease at play within her. "This way, my lord."

To her surprise, Lord Harrington was quiet as they climbed the steps, which was possibly because he was concentrating on not missing a stair. It was something of a difficult task, and Sophie found herself taking the strain of his weight on more than one occasion, but eventually they reached the hallway.

"The library first, I think," Sophie said, hoping that he might allow her to return to the servants' quarters once he was settled in front of the fire. "I am quite sure there is some brandy to be had in there." Why he had not thought to go in search of it there first instead of rummaging around in the pantry, she did not know – although mayhap being a little the worse for wear did not always give clarity to one's senses. Why he thought he needed more was another question entirely.

"Here we are," she said, opening the door to the library and allowing him to step inside before her. "I believe there is brandy in the corner."

Much to her shock, Lord Harrington grasped her around

the waist, steadying himself before looking deeply into her eyes.

"I find my need for brandy has slowly begun to diminish," he murmured, one hand catching her chin and brushing her skin gently. "In its place, I find another need growing."

A cloying fear began to climb up her throat, suddenly recalling all of the times she had been caught by her cousin.

"No, my lord," she said, firmly, trying to step back from him. "I am not that kind of woman."

He frowned and lessened his grip but did not let her go. "You intrigue me, Sarah," he said, quietly, his eyes searching her face. "What is it about you that puzzles me so?"

She found herself entirely unable to answer, her fear beginning to recede as her memories of Malcolm were replaced by her emotions in the present moment with Lord Harrington. There was a difference between him and Malcolm, for he was not holding her in an aggressive manner, was not demanding that she disrobe for him. However, she could not forget what the rest of the staff had told her about his reputation.

"I think I should go, my lord," she said quietly, stepping away from him and he let his arm fall from her side. "There is brandy on the tray by the fire, so you shall not be without, although I would suggest that perhaps you have had enough for tonight."

She clapped a hand over her mouth, realizing what she had said. The words had come out before she had remembered her station here, and she could only hope he would forget her forwardness as she made to make for the door, only for his hand to catch hers.

When she turned to face him, she saw a curious expression on his face, as though he was not quite sure why he had stopped her. However there was no terror filling her, no desperate need to run and hide from him.

"Sarah," he whispered softly before stepping forward, gently cupping her cheek, and, pausing for a moment, he gave her time to step away. For a reason even unbeknownst to her, however she stayed in place.

Then he bent his head to kiss her.

CHAPTER 11

"Good morning, my lord!"

Benjamin groaned and flung one hand over his face, only for a shirt button to catch him in the corner of the eye. Letting out a yelp of surprise, he blinked wildly and looked about him, surprised to discover that he was in the library.

"I see you discovered more brandy, after all," the butler commented, clicking his fingers to a maid, who brought in a tray stocked with coffee, toast, and pastries. "I was told all rooms required refilling. I am sorry you felt it lacking. I shall make sure all the decanters are prepared for this evening."

"Thank you," Benjamin rasped, feeling as though he'd swallowed a mouthful of gravel. He tried to sit up, mortified to discover that he had fallen asleep on the chaise lounge, one of his legs dangling off the side. His head began to ache as he came into a sitting position, and he wondered if the smell of alcohol was from the room or from his person.

"A bath, I think," he muttered, as the butler poured the coffee. "What time is it?"

"Past midday," the butler replied, in a slightly cheerful

tone. Benjamin couldn't decide whether or not the servant was subtly mocking him. "The bath is being prepared as we speak."

Benjamin wanted to comment on the butler's cheerfulness and efficiency, only to stop himself just in time. The man was doing his job and doing it well.

"Thank you," he muttered, after a moment. "I shall be up presently."

The butler nodded and began to leave the room, only for a sudden thought to hit Benjamin. "I am expecting my guests tomorrow afternoon, I believe," he said, making the butler pause. "Is everything prepared?"

"It is indeed," the butler replied. "We have the blue room and purple room ready for your guests."

"Good," Benjamin said, quietly. "Make sure everything is arranged. I want a marvellous dinner prepared for their arrival tomorrow." Remembering that Sarah was due to continue her work in his study, he waved one arm. "Oh, and tell Sarah to continue with the accounts today. She should know what to do."

There was a momentary pause before the butler clicked his heels together, bowed, and excused himself. Benjamin chewed slowly on a piece of hot buttered toast, already beginning to feel a little better. Taking another sip of his coffee, he frowned as he looked around the room, wondering what on earth he'd done last evening.

He could remember feeling miserable, missing his friends and pastimes in London, and so had – foolishly or otherwise – begun to lose himself in liquor. Unfortunately, his brandy had been in short supply in the study and so… what had he done then?

His brow furrowed. He could not remember for the life of him, although he was quite sure that he had managed to make his way below stairs for whatever reason. Swallowing his toast, he made to pick up another piece, only for ice to suddenly fill his veins, freezing him in place.

Sarah.

Sarah had been there.

A groan escaped his lips as he put his head in his hands, his toast and coffee immediately forgotten. What had he done?

His fingers touched a spot on his cheek, feeling a small bruise beneath his fingers. The sudden memory of Sarah slapping him, hard, came straight into his mind, and he groaned aloud again.

Everything came back at once, hazy but clear. He had tried to kiss Sarah. A member of his household staff, who had been doing nothing more than what was expected of her He had tried to press his attentions on her, as, of course, many masters did. However, he had promised himself he would not be that kind of man, despite the recent lack of company in his bed.

The truth was, he was desperately attracted to the maid, perhaps all the more because he wouldn't allow himself to have her. Although he felt it was much more than that. She had a great number of feminine qualities, and her graceful-ness and gentleness made him think of her as a lady, even though he knew she could never be such a thing. She was unlike any servant he had come across before, particularly given her skills in arithmetic. Her elegant handwriting flowed, and her careful manner in all things lifted her high in his estimation. Why, then, had he done something as foolish as attempt to kiss her?

Then again, she was a servant and that meant that she should not have struck him. To do so would mean instant dismissal, but Benjamin could not bring himself to send her away without a reference. That would be cruelty in itself, for it was not her fault that he had behaved in such a way. Was she simply to accept his attentions, no matter how unwanted, in order to keep her position?

A great many gentlemen would say so, said the small voice in the back of his mind.

"No!" Benjamin exclaimed aloud, thumping his fist on the table. "I am not going to be that kind of master!"

It was not only his father's edict that hung over his head, Benjamin realized, but rather a slow-growing desire to be known as a gentleman that did right by his staff. He did not want to become a hard-hearted, cruel tyrant, but rather a careful, considerate master. It would make his father proud, yes, but Benjamin wanted to be that kind of gentleman for himself, rather than for his father.

Besides that, Sarah had left her previous employment because of such a man. He vowed to be better than that.

Pushing himself up from the chair, Benjamin swayed for a moment, lights going off in his head. His head began to pound once more, but Benjamin gritted his teeth and continued toward the door regardless. Now was not the time to indulge himself and his own pain. He would have to find Sarah and speak to her privately. Goodness knows what was going through her head. She was probably terrified that he was about to throw her from his house, given that she had struck him. He wanted to ease that at once.

Hoping that he did not look too disheveled, Benjamin made his way back toward the study, hoping that Sarah was there already as the butler should have instructed. Pushing open the door, he saw that she was sitting at her small writing desk in the corner, her face pale as it lifted to his the moment he stepped inside.

"Oh, my lord," she breathed, her face almost milk white as she rose. He saw that her hands were trembling as she intertwined her fingers, her mouth a worried line. "Good morning."

"Good morning, Sarah," he grunted, wondering how to explain himself to someone who was, in fact, a servant in his household. "Thank you for being so diligent in your work."

She glanced up at him, fear in her eyes. "My lord, I must apologize for – "

"You will apologize for nothing," he said, firmly, seeing her mouth fall open in surprise. "I have only just recalled how I have behaved and I must confess that I am ashamed of it."

He watched her closely, seeing her blink furiously as her cheeks suddenly burned with heat. There were deep circles under her eyes, smudges of blue and grey that told him she had not slept well. Had she been worried that he would send her from the house? It was evident that she had not been expecting him to speak to her in such a way, but had rather been waiting for him to rail at her or give her notice.

"You were very good to me, were you not?" he continued, ignoring the spiralling heat in his core that spread up into his chest as he recalled just how close her mouth had been to his. "You brought me back up the stairs and into the library. I do not know why I was below but I — "

"You were in search of brandy, my lord."

Shame filled him. "I see," he said, thickly. "Well, I thank you for your help."

"I should not have struck you as I did," Sarah said after a moment, her voice breathless. "I… I simply reacted. I did not know what else to do."

Benjamin closed his eyes for a moment, seeing just how badly his actions had affected her. "I was wrong to do what I did," he said, quietly. "I am aware that many gentlemen treat their staff in whatever way they wish, but I will not be that man. My father expects it and I find that I am beginning to expect it of myself."

"Your father?" she echoed, a curious look on her face as

she stood and stepped closer to him. "Why– " Remembering herself and her position, she covered her mouth with her hand, looking quite horrified. "Oh, my lord, I do beg your pardon," she exclaimed, her cheeks growing quite a becoming pink. "You just looked quite grave and I wanted to ease your –- "

"Have no fear," he muttered, surprised to discover that he wanted to share all with her. "I can see that you are settled and so I shall leave you to your work."

She smiled, albeit something of a watery one, relief filling her expression. "You are very good, my lord," she said, softly. "I thank you for your kindness."

Benjamin did not know what to say, wanting to repeat the very same sentiments back to her. Oh, how much she had put up with from him. He was caught for a moment by her loveliness, thinking just how kind her expression was. It was as if she saw him for what he truly was, and had simply forgiven him for his actions toward her.

"I shall leave you now," he muttered, stepping away toward the door. He glanced back at her, seeing her dark head already bent over her work. His heart pounded strangely within him as he took a breath, settled his shoulders and left the study. He was more than ready for his bath.

CHAPTER 12

*S*ophie continued with her work, trying not to think of all that had taken place and instead focused on the task at hand.

However, she could think of nothing else besides her most recent conversation with Lord Harrington. Putting down her quill, she let out a frustrated sigh and rose from her chair.

Wandering to the window, Sophie hugged her arms tightly around herself, wondering what was to become of her. She had been terrified that Lord Harrington would remove her from her position in his household and had worried over where she would go from here. She refused to ever return to her cousin's manor.

When Lord Harrington had leaned in to kiss her, Sophie had been so shocked that she'd briefly allowed his lips to touch hers, but a raging fear had suddenly taken a hold of her and, without even intending to, she had struck him across the face. He had staggered back, one hand going to the reddening mark on his cheek, his eyes widening in shock, and she had collapsed, horrified, against the wall. Her limbs had turned to wood, her body growing heavy with the weight of what she'd done – and, somehow, she'd found the strength to leave. She'd stumbled her way back to her room, her hand at her mouth as quiet sobs escaped her.

When the morning came without any note of the incident, Sophie had not known what to think. She had wondered whether if, in his drunken state, he had forgotten about the incident entirely, but then she thought perhaps he simply intended to rail at her alone, in the study. With no other choice but to do as requested, she had sat alone in her mahogany armchair and waited for Lord Harrington to return.

His words to her were the exact opposite of what she had expected. To see him so apologetic, so remorseful, had made her heart lighten, relief pouring into her very soul. He was not like her cousin, treating others just as he pleased without a thought for their feelings. He had also let her leave without question last night, unlike Malcolm, who would have been enraged by her slap. Yet, at the same time, Sophie knew that this was something Lord Harrington was well used to doing. A gentleman of his fortune and title would take his pleasures where he wanted, although she was relieved he appeared to have some kind of respect for his staff. The way he had apologized to her proved as much.

Looking out at the view of the forest in the distance, Sophie sighed. She had not meant to ask him what he meant by his father's expectations, but the pained expression on his face had caused a great swell of sympathy to rise up within her, and the question had escaped her mouth almost of its own accord.

"Foolish, foolish girl," she murmured to herself, her hands falling to her sides as she stepped away from the window. She should have nothing but respect for Lord Harrington, given that he was the master of the house and she apparently a mere servant. To show feelings of sympathy for him could not be wise, even though her imprudent heart yearned to know more about him. When his lips had touched hers, she had reacted in a way that had come from months of living in fear, pursued by a man who cared nothing for her – but now, she saw that Lord Harrington was, at the very least, trying to be both a respectful and considerate master. Her regard for him grew as she considered his apology, her fingers briefly touching her lips as she recalled how he had touched them with his own, ever so briefly.

Sophie had never been kissed before, but she suddenly discovered that the thought of Lord Harrington doing such a thing again sent a shower of sparks down her spine — not of fear, but a new emotion, one that equally scared and excited her. She could never allow herself to give into these feelings, of course, particularly given that he had no awareness of her true identity. Her feelings confused her, her stomach beginning to swirl with a mixture of anxiety and desire. Sophie looked back at the desk where the accounts awaited her, her eyes unseeing, struggling to put an order to her thoughts.

What if I told him the truth?

The thought was sharp, making her gasp. Her eyes widened as she considered telling him who she was, and wondered what he might do in return. Would he allow her to continue here, in her position? Would he return her to her cousin, refusing to get mixed up in the situation? She could not imagine that he would do such a thing but, then again, she did not know him particularly well. Perhaps if their acquaintance increased then she might feel able to confide in him.

Living as she was at this present moment was all fine and good, but, in the long term, Sophie had very little idea of what she could do. Would she continue to draw a salary from Lord Harrington until her cousin died? That might not be for a great many years, and she would be old and gray by then, still without access to her fortune, and she certainly wouldn't find a husband in her current situation. She frowned, pressing one hand to her temple as her head began to ache. If only her father had not determined that she must marry in order to receive her inheritance.

"I shall take one day at a time," she murmured to herself, sitting again and trying to focus on her work. She would worry about the future later. For the moment, she had a job to do and she would be content with that. Perhaps circumstances would change, or something would occur that might alter her path in some way. No matter what happened, Sophie determined to remain both satisfied and productive. If it was necessary for the truth to come out at some point, then she would worry about that at the time, not before. It would do her no good to give any thought to such anxiety now.

Sophie worked in silence for some time, frowning to herself as she spotted another tiny, yet important error. There appeared to be a small amount missing from the calculations. It was not frequent, and therefore could easily escape someone's notice, but it was there all the same. Her frown deepened as she noted the error down, realizing that it was now the fifth such mistake she had discovered in the last two months' accounts. Surely that was a little unusual.

"I see you are hard at work as always."

Starting in surprise, Sophie looked up to see Lord Harrington smiling down at her, having entered and even closed the door without her becoming aware of him. She must learn to be more observant of her surroundings. She had a tendency to get lost in her task.

"Oh, yes, my lord. Of course. There is a lot to do." Her face burned as she wondered if it sounded as though she were complaining. "Not that it is too much, of course. That is not what I mean. I – "

Lord Harrington laughed aloud and held up his hand, his eyes twinkling at her. "You need not worry yourself so, Sarah. I know what you are intending to say. I am sure you are making very good progress."

Managing to catch her breath and still fighting the growing heat in her cheeks, Sophie tried to smile. "Thank you, my lord." Goodness, just seeing him again made her flustered. His warmth toward her was a little more increased from yesterday, and Sophie supposed it was in an attempt to calm any further worries she might have over a potential dismissal.

"My lord, would you like…" she didn't quite know how to make the offer to him without insulting him.

"Yes?" he asked, tilting his head to the side in question as the ocean of his eyes bore into hers.

"Would you like me to try to help you understand the accounts a bit better?" she looked up at him, hesitation in her voice, unsure of how he might respond.

"I would," he said with a grin, putting her at ease. "Though I must tell you the chance of me understanding anything, no matter how good of a teacher you are, is quite low. Many a tutor attempted to teach me, but none found much success."

She picked up the ledgers and made to carry them to his desk when he took them from her. She felt the heat of his fingers as they brushed hers. He moved the smaller armchair around the desk to place it beside him.

"Well," she said. "We shall begin with the importance of entering the correct cost to each item, which has been noted in this column. Beside that are the quantities. I have been noting whether the calculations have been completed correctly for the sum total and then finally the additions of each column for the weekly and monthly totals."

He followed her finger as she pointed to the page in front of her.

"I understand that part," he said with a smile. "It's the calculations which I have trouble with."

"Very well," she said, nodding her head.

She pulled out a blank sheet of parchment and began to slowly explain a simple equation. He nodded in understanding, and when she provided him with a similar one to complete, he proved capable of solving it.

"Very good," she said with a smile, before moving to something more complicated.

They continued for quite some time, and Sophie was pleased with his progress. He listened to what she said, though she stumbled over her words when his eyes met hers or she sensed his nearness. Now and then she could pick up the scent that was uniquely him — the pine of the forest he rode in, and the slight hint of brandy on his breath.

He completed a more complicated calculation, and she looked up at him with a smile on her lips to find his face very near, and very serious, his mouth hovering just above hers.

"Sarah?" he breathed, as if in question, likely as to whether she would slap him once more if he tried anything. In answer she leaned up and closed the gap between them, her lips reaching up to softly press against his, surprising herself as much as him.

CHAPTER 13

*B*enjamin let the kiss linger there for a moment, before he slowly began to move his lips against hers, asking for just slightly more without wanting to scare her away. She responded not with any sort of fear or hesitancy, but rather a wanting of her own. She breathed a soft sigh against his lips, which proved his undoing.

He put an arm around her to find a better angle, lifting her small frame effortlessly to sit her on his lap. His strong arm held her close, and she reached her hands up to tangle in his hair, pushing it back from his forehead.

He teased her lips with his tongue, and when she opened for him, he eased it into her soft mouth, stroking her lovingly. She kissed him back with equal measure, both shocking and pleasing him. His hands roamed over her sides, feeling the curves he knew would be there under that garish maid's uniform. He broke from her lips, and was kissing his way down her neck when she gave a moan of pleasure, bringing him to his senses and breaking him from the spell.

He gently picked her up from his lap, setting her back

down in her chair beside him. "I — I apologize, Sarah, I should not have done that."

"If apologizing must be done, then I believe I was equally at fault, my lord," she said, looking up at him with a soft smile.

My lord. The address reminded him of the fact that he was taking advantage of a woman in his employ, one of the very things he had promised his father — and himself — he would not do. He was still drinking too much, taking liberties with a woman he should not have, and relying on said maid to make sense of his ledgers. He sighed. He was not making much progress.

"Are you happy with your work, Sarah?" he asked her as he stood abruptly and began pacing the room.

"Yes, my lord," she responded with a nod, bemused.

"Do you feel it has been... appropriate for you to be working on the books of this estate?" he asked, though why he was asking the maid this, he had no idea.

"I confess from my knowledge it is highly irregular, my lord, but I do not see the harm in it," she said, her level gaze open and questioning.

"Perhaps I can find a position for you besides a maid," he said. "It seems a rather strange title for you considering you have scarcely undertaken any of the usual duties of a maid — a bookkeeper perhaps? I shall have to think on it."

She simply nodded her head. "I am happy with whatever you deem best, my lord," she said.

*　*　*

THE CONVERSATION WAS SOMEWHAT STRANGE, but Sophie had learned to expect the unexpected with Lord Harrington. Like that kiss. He had given her every opportunity to walk away from it, and yet she had wanted it — craved it, even. When his face was just a breath away from hers, she could not help but lean in, to see what he tasted like. What they shared had left her breathless, and even now she was having difficulty concentrating on what he was saying.

"Have you anything to report on the accounts?" he asked, walking back over to his desk. "Anything I need to know about?"

Sophie paused for a moment, unsure of whether she should note the issue as of yet. "I am not quite sure, my lord."

"That sounds ominous," he commented, his eyebrows lifting in surprise. "Something wrong?"

Trying her best to explain without going into too much detail, Sophie gave a slight shake of her head. "There may be an issue, but I have yet to decide whether it is worth bringing it to your attention. It may simply be some poor accounting."

His face lost its smile. "Well, do let me know whenever you decide, Sarah. I trust your judgement of course, but regardless I should like to know what has caused you to worry, even if it proves to be nothing."

Sophie blinked, taken aback by his compliment. It was as if, just for a moment, he was speaking to her as though she were an equal in his eyes. There was a sudden, desperate urge to tell him the truth, but before she could even open her mouth, there came a knock on the door. Sophie discreetly rose and returned to her desk in the corner, making herself nearly invisible.

"Yes?" Lord Harrington asked, as the butler walked in, a note in his hand.

"This just came for you, my lord."

Sophie tried not to appear interested, remembering that she was not meant to be doing anything other than the accounts. She began to mentally calculate another equation, trying her best to ignore everything else.

"Ah, 'tis nothing," Lord Harrington muttered. "It is just

Lord Dunstable. He is going to be a day later than he thought. Something about a relative of his." He shrugged and discarded the note. "So it will just be Lord Haversham tomorrow, and Lord Dunstable the day after."

The butler nodded, enquired as to whether his master needed anything else and, on being dismissed, closed the door behind him.

A drop of sweat fell from Sophie's brow and landed on the parchment, blurring the ink. The moment she had heard Lord Harrington mutter her cousin's name, she had turned into a terrified, frantic mess.

Her hands trembled so badly that she was forced to put down her quill, managing to somehow tip the inkwell. Ink spread all over the parchment she had been working on, although thankfully the accounts were not damaged. Managing to steady the inkwell, Sophie drew in a shaky breath and attempted to rise to her feet. Her legs had no strength as she struggled to stand, her hands clutching the sides of the desk.

"Excuse me, my lord," she managed to say in a somewhat breathless voice. "I – I'm sorry, I didn't mean to, I..." She trailed off, gesturing at the spilt ink. "Let me get a rag."

Lord Harrington did not seem in the least perturbed, simply shrugging as he rose to his feet. He picked up the parchment, skillfully managing not to drop a single spot of ink, and threw the entire thing in the fire.

"Nothing to worry about," he said, cheerfully, as though everything was at right. "Just a few small splashes to clean up." He walked back to sit at his desk, leaving her to clean up the remaining drops.

Sophie closed her eyes for a moment, trying to steady herself. She simply had to get herself out of this room and away from him so that she might have a few moments in which to reclaim her senses. Her limbs were heavy, and her lack of strength made it difficult to even move them.

"Is everything quite all right?"

"Yes, yes," Sophie murmured, trying and failing to put a smile on her face. "I am just a little embarrassed, that is all. Do excuse me."

Lord Harrington regarded her for another moment before turning his attention back to his correspondence. Managing not to be sick, Sophie made her way to the door, her hand shaking so badly that she could barely grasp the door handle.

"Are you quite sure all is well?"

Sophie could not look back at him, afraid she was going to burst into a flood of tears, from which could stem a great deal of confusion.

Tell him the truth.

Once again, the small, insistent voice in the back of her mind prodded her to do what she could, to beg him to save her from her cousin. Her hand slipped as she tried to turn the door handle, her palms too sweaty to grip it.

"Might I talk to you, my lord?" she whispered, wiping her hand on her dress as surreptitiously as she could. She managed to twist her head just enough to look back at him, seeing him study her with some concern.

"Yes, of course, Sarah," he replied. "About the accounts, is it? Or is it about… what we shared?"

He still thought she was upset about either the kiss or what she had found and, at the present moment, she could not find the words to tell him anything else. Besides that, clearly he was good friends with Malcolm, having invited him to his home. Oh, what were the chances? Her heart was pained in her chest, her body still shaking with fear at seeing her cousin again. She could hardly speak as she told herself to breathe deeply. Stars spotted in her vision, warning her that she was close to fainting.

Finally, the door handle turned beneath her fingers. "The accounts," she managed to say, quite flustered by now and simply needing to escape. "It can wait."

"Later then," he said, as though he were having quite an ordinary conversation, unable to see her distress for anything more than being puzzled about something in the accounts. "I am due to go out to visit my tenants this afternoon, so I shall speak to you later this evening."

Sophie did not respond, even though she knew she ought to. She could not talk to him now, not when her mind was all of a muddle and her composure more than lacking. She would need to have a calm mind were she to tell him everything with clarity.

Managing to slip out of the door and shut it behind her, Sophie found strength from somewhere, forcing herself to move forward. She could not exactly collapse in a heap in the hallway, only to be found by Lord Harrington or one of the servants, who she was finally winning over with kindness. *Get yourself together, girl*, she told herself. Gritting her teeth and trying her best to control her shaking, Sophie forced her legs to move. They took her to the servants' stairs and then down below into the kitchen where she finally felt safe. She collapsed at the table, putting her head on her arms and taking deep breaths. She steadied herself as she tried to determine whatever she was to do now.

CHAPTER 14

*B*y the time Sophie managed to regain her composure, both the cook and the housekeeper had found her in the kitchen, horrified to find her in such a state. Sophie attempted to reassure them that all was well, only her tears began to fall once more when the cook hugged her.

The words tumbled from her mouth, her devastation at Malcolm's pending arrival apparent. The housekeeper, Mrs. Martins, looked distressed, although her expression grew resolute as Sophie spoke.

"You shall simply have to stay hidden away from him," she declared when Sophie had finished her story. "He doesn't know you are here. We shall make sure you are not to be in his presence at any time."

"But Lord Harrington – "

"Lord Harrington will have no opportunity to request your presence in any sphere other than that in which you are already in," Mrs. Martins interrupted, putting a firm hand on Sophie's shoulder. "He has made good use of you, to the point that I see very little of you. I should be very surprised if he expected you to do as the other maids do, just because he has guests!"

"And they will not be in his study either, I should say," Mrs. Potts continued, quietly, her eyes ablaze with sympathy. "The study is for work and Lord Harrington will not be working when his two friends are present, that is for certain."

"You shall find yourself quite alone for the most part, I believe," Mrs. Martins finished, evidently trying to be encouraging. "And, if you are to have company in the study, it will just be Lord Harrington and not his two companions. Gentlemen have no reason to enter another man's study, not unless they wish to aid him in his work in some way – and, believe me, that is not why your cousin and Lord Haversham are coming."

Sophie drew in a deep breath or two, her heartbeat slowly returning to normal. "Yes, I can see that now," she replied, as Mrs. Potts hurried away to start making up a tea tray for her. "But I am still filled with dread, knowing that he will be here." She took a steadying breath, pushing down the panic that threatened to fill her. "I have nowhere else to go, otherwise nothing could induce me to stay here, despite how kind you have all been to me."

The housekeeper patted her hand gently. "It is most unfortunate, I confess, but we will do what we can to keep you safe."

Mrs. Potts put the teapot on the table, and Sophie smiled gratefully as the steaming brew was poured.

"I had thought of telling Lord Harrington everything," she confessed, once they were all seated. "If he knows all, then he might be able to help me."

Both the housekeeper and the cook looked more than a little astonished at the suggestion but, after exchanging a glance, Mrs. Martins began to nod, slowly.

"It may be a good idea," she murmured, after a time. "However, the only thing I would caution is that your cousin is obviously Lord Harrington's friend. Do you think Lord Harrington would be inclined to believe you over him?"

The thought gave Sophie pause, for it was her same fear.

"My cousin never spoke of any of his acquaintances to me," she confessed, pressing one hand to her brow. "I cannot tell how close they might be. Nor do I know Lord Harrington particularly well but, should he discover that I have lied to him without confessing to it, then I think he might very well be more angry with me than if I told him all when I had the opportunity."

Mrs. Potts bit her lip. "We cannot advise you in this, my dear. Only you can make that choice."

"But we will do whatever we can to assist you, no matter what you choose," Mrs. Martins added, with a smile of encouragement. "You have done a wonderful job thus far and I know that Lord Harrington is pleased with your work."

Sophie drew in a long breath and let it out slowly. It was time to return to that work. "I must go," she said, quietly, getting to her feet. "I know Lord Harrington is out but he requested I continue with the accounts."

"And we have much to be getting on with here also," Mrs. Martins said, briskly, also rising. "Do come and talk to me again if you need to do so, Miss Carmichael."

"I thank you," Sophie replied, her voice a little hoarse as she looked at the two ladies who had proven to be dear friends in such a short time. "You must call me Sophie. You are both so very good to me."

* * *

AND SO IT WAS THAT, many hours later, Sophie found herself still working hard on the accounts. Lord Harrington had not returned to his study and she had only taken a short break to eat with the rest of the household staff. She had caught the concerned glances of both Mrs. Martins and Mrs. Potts but had smiled in response, pretending that all was well, even though her stomach churned every time she so much as thought about her cousin.

The accounts, however, gave her something to think and focus on, instead of Lord Dunstable. There were these small, intricate errors that seemed to regularly occur. The transactions were not always particularly large ones, but, when Sophie compared them to the receipts Lord Harrington had given her, she found inconsistencies. The receipts were for a smaller amount than the accounts showed were paid for by the estate, which could only mean one thing. Whoever was doing these transactions was taking a few extra coins for themselves.

Her heart grew heavy as she noted yet another discrepancy. This was no mistake. This was a regular event, and obviously whoever it was had hoped not to be discovered.

Clearly, with the Harrington master away from the estate for a prolonged period of time, it meant that the thief had become a little bolder as the months went on. Instead of the transactions taking place once every two months or so, they began to increase to once a month and lately even twice. Sophie could not account for the losses otherwise.

The door opened and, much to Sophie's surprise given the hour, in walked Lord Harrington – who looked just as astonished to see her as she was to see him.

"My, you are working late," he mumbled, stepping inside and closing the door. "I know I pay you, Sarah, but this is beyond your requirements. It is gone midnight!"

"Is it?" Sophie asked, surprised. "I hadn't noticed. I did want to talk to you, my lord, but it can wait until the morning."

"Oh yes," he said at once, his eyes widening a little. "The accounts. You are fastidious."

Sophie could not help but blush at the compliment, despite his incorrect assumptions.

"I have a great deal to learn from you, I think," he continued, walking toward the large Bergere chair by the fire. "Come, Sarah. Sit here for a moment and tell me what you have found."

Sophie did as he asked, walking toward, staring into its orange blaze as she thought of what she should say. She wanted to tell him that, while she did want to discuss the accounts, she had something of an even greater importance to share with him him, but she could not quite find the words. She thought on what Mrs. Potts had suggested, on him being friends with her cousin. He indicated the comfortable matching chair to his left, and she found her legs a little wobbly as she sat down.

Once more, she felt as if he were treating her like an equal, even though he probably had no intention to do such a thing and was simply lonely, requiring someone to talk to.

"How do you find the stamina to focus on a thing as boring as the accounts for such a prolonged period of time?" he asked, taking the sheaf of papers from her hands and setting them on the table between them.

Sophie laughed softly. "Because I must, my lord," she answered, still smiling. "You cannot think that I have anything else to entertain me or to distract me from my work."

He shifted uncomfortably in his chair. "No," he muttered, passing one hand through his hair. "No, I suppose not. You do very well, Sarah. As you know, I find it difficult to concentrate on such things at the best of times."

"You seem to be catching onto it. You will improve with time," she promised, seeing the flush of embarrassment in his cheeks. "After all, I believe this is your first time running an estate?"

Lord Harrington's eyes shifted to hers, a small, wry smile tugging at his lips. "The staff are talking about what a failure I am, I suppose."

"No, not in the least!" she protested, leaning forward in her chair. "They are saying no such thing, my lord."

He snorted. "You cannot expect me to believe that they do not talk of me, Sarah. It is good of you to try to protect them – and to protect me in doing so." Something in his eyes flickered. "You are very good. Too good."

Sophie's mouth went dry as he caught her hand, squeezing it lightly. Her heart began to quicken in her chest, beating so loudly she was sure he could hear it. She had no fear, no dread that he would force himself on her as her cousin might. When they had kissed this afternoon, he had waited for her. She knew he would only take what was freely given. She found in herself there continued to be a deep-rooted desire growing for him.

"Please don't slap me again for my forwardness," he rumbled, dropping her hand and sitting back with a somewhat rueful smile on his face. "I should not have touched you again. In fact, I should not have any such feelings for you, Sarah." He groaned and shook his head, passing a hand over his eyes. "I should not even be *speaking* to you in such a way…." His voice trailed away, his expression confused.

"I – I want to be of assistance to you," she answered softly, her heart going out to him. "I can see that there are things that trouble you but you have no one to speak to." Realizing that she was being too bold, she pressed her lips together and tried to smile. "Although I am sure your companions will be a great comfort to you." She wanted to determine his closeness to Malcolm, to decide whether she should broach the subject of the nature of her true identity.

"They will be very little help, I assure you," Lord Harrington muttered with a low chuckle, shaking his head. "I have been looking forward to their company, but I do not think they will be of very great assistance, I must confess."

"Oh?" Sophie asked, unable to help herself. "I thought they might aid you with some of the more difficult aspects of running the estate."

He laughed softly. "You think too well of people, Sarah. When I invited them here, at first I thought perhaps they would have advice for me, but I am realizing that will not be the case and I was simply creating an excuse for myself. No, they are men who enjoy the pleasures of life and... well, as you likely are aware, I am one of those men, though I am trying to change as of recently. I would have remained the same if it were not that certain circumstances — which I shall not embarrass myself by telling you of — required me to leave town. If my father had not forced this situation on to me, then I would not be here now." Lifting his brandy glass to his mouth, he took a large draught while Sophie waited for him to continue.

"I should not judge them for I am just like them. I am not a good man, Sarah," he finished, looking down at his glass. "Yet, I am trying to be. I want to mend my ways and to prove to my father that I can be a man who is respected by others. However, I fear the task may be too great for me to overcome. My friends, while good company, will most likely attempt to pull me from my responsibilities and return to a life of frivolity, even on my own estate."

Sophie saw the confusion in his eyes, the pain in his expression, and could do nothing other than reach forward to take his hand, even though she knew she ought not to be doing anything of the sort, but rather should be staying far away from him. Her compassionate heart, however, yearned to bring him comfort, to assure him that he was not the man he feared he was.

"No, my lord, do not say such things," she exclaimed, her eyes focusing on his, which now regarded her in surprise. "I have seen you struggle to do what you must, even though I know you find the accounts particularly complex. You have shown remorse and done exactly what is expected of you in visiting your tenants and already beginning to plan improvements. You are of strong character. No matter what your companions wish of you, I know you will be able to withstand such lures. Your determination does you credit, my lord. Do not think so little of yourself, I beg of you."

His expression grew pained, as though he was struggling to accept what she said. Sophie kept her grip on his hand, doing her best to ignore the tingling that was already beginning to spread up her arm. She wanted nothing more than to bring him a little comfort, to encourage him to believe in his own strong character.

"I will be here whenever you wish to talk, my lord," she finished, her voice barely louder than a whisper. "I know it is not my place, but–"

"It *is* your place," he rumbled, placing his other hand over hers. "My goodness, Sarah, your presence alone brings me more comfort than I could ever imagine. I think I shall have to keep you here with me forever." His lips lifted in a small smile, making Sophie catch her breath.

"I am being too forward," she murmured, making to pull her hand back. "Forgive me, my lord."

"There is nothing to forgive, Sarah," he whispered, refusing to allow her to leave him. He leaned his head back against the chair, letting out a long, frustrated breath. "Your gentle spirit simply adds to your loveliness." He looked back at her, his fingers lifting to brush her cheek. "Whatever am I to do with you?"

Sophie could not stop herself from rising from her chair and coming closer to him. When he tugged her onto his lap, she went willingly, her heart thundering in her chest and causing her to breathe in short gasps. She should not be doing this. She should not be allowing herself to become so caught up, particularly when he did not know the truth about who she was.

"My dear Sarah," he murmured, his eyes burning into her soul. "Slap me again if you wish, but I find I cannot help myself."

Sophie could not answer and, when his lips pressed against hers, she felt herself melt into his arms. She let him draw her head back and angle her toward him, feeling as though she were clay in the hands of a master potter. Heat seared her skin as she wound her hands around his neck and, as he began to pull the pins from her hair, Sophie drew him closer, not wanting this moment to end.

CHAPTER 15

*B*enjamin could not explain the great swell of emotion that was coursing through him as he ran his hands through Sarah's long, dark curls. This was more heated than their innocent kiss that afternoon and, while certainly far from his first kiss, somehow, he had never experienced the likes of this before.

He had always appreciated women, but only for what they could offer him in the moment. They enjoyed one another, and then he was happy to be on his way.

With Sarah, it was not so.

He admired her. Even though she was a servant and therefore under his control, the respect he held for her bordered on admiration. Her compassionate heart shone through in almost every word she said. Her kindness toward him when he had been drunk and improper had brought a healing to his soul. Her loveliness of both face and character continued to pull him in, even though he was trying his best to resist.

But that he could not seem to do.

Having seen the light in her eyes, the pink of her cheeks

and the darting of her gaze toward his lips, Benjamin had taken a chance and given in to his feelings. Hauling her into her arms, he had pressed gentle kisses to her mouth, and she returned them with equal fervor.

It was clear she lacked experience with a man, but that shy vulnerability made his heart soar. He wanted to show her the depths of love making, although inwardly, Benjamin swore to himself that he would not take her innocence. He could not, *would* not be that man again. Not when Sarah herself had such faith in him.

His body began to grow hot with need, his fingers tracing the curve of her neck as she gasped against his lips. With a great force of will, Benjamin made himself move slowly, pushing back his overwhelming desire for her. This was not to be the same experience he had shared so many other willing women. This was different. Sarah was different.

With gentle fingers, he undid one of the buttons on the back of her dress, needing to see more than her blasted uniform would allow. Managing to free her shoulder from its confines, he began to feather kisses down the column of her throat and along her collarbone, hearing her gasp aloud. Her fingers dragged themselves through his hair and she arched back as though desperate for more of his caresses.

"Sarah," he breathed, sitting up so that he might look into her eyes. "You are so very beautiful."

Her eyes fluttered open, her lips parting in surprise. "Thank you, my lord."

"Benjamin," he murmured, brushing her hair at her temples. "You must call me Benjamin."

She blinked then as if drawn from the warmth of their embrace back to cold reality.

"No," she stammered, sitting up a little higher and tugging at the shoulder of her dress. "No, I should not. This is all wrong. I should not be– "

"I have nothing but the best of intentions for you, I promise," Benjamin said, hurriedly, suddenly afraid that she was about to leave him. "Sarah, I mean it. Call me what you wish, but I am trying to be a changed man and I find with you that I...."

She looked at him, no longer struggling to remove herself from him. "What is it?" she asked, softly. "Tell me, please. I must know what you feel."

To tell her was to make himself vulnerable to her but the desire to have her stay with him was stronger than his reluctance. "I find that I feel more for you than I have ever felt before," he whispered, the truth tearing at his heart. "I do not know what I shall do with it, nor what lies ahead for us, but I will not allow myself to use you and then throw you aside. I want to know what it means to care for another."

Sarah did not respond, her mouth forming a perfect circle as she gazed at him in astonishment.

"I do not know whether you can trust me, given my previous behavior," he continued, more quietly. "But I mean it, truly. I feel things for you that I want to explore."

"I am a servant and I have much to lose," she replied, anxiety in her expression although she did not move away.

He shook his head. "I shall never let anything happen to your reputation. I swear it," he replied, desperate to convince her that he meant every word.

"There can be no future for us," she whispered, a sheen of tears in her eyes. "Despite what I feel, I cannot allow this to continue past... past tonight."

Benjamin did not allow her to proceed, pressing his mouth to hers once more. She responded immediately, more familiar with him now. Unable to stop himself, Benjamin ran his tongue along the seam of her lips, pressing inside when she opened them. Emboldened, she clung to him fervently, returning his kiss as best she could.

Heat roared in his chest, bursting through his veins. Benjamin found the back of her dress once more and began to undo more buttons, and, much to his surprise, he discovered that she was doing the same to his shirt. This was not what he had expected, nor intended.

Her hands touched the bare skin of his chest, her cool fingers running over him boldly. Oh, how he wanted to explain what he felt, how he desired to have her in his arms for the rest of the night – but instead, he simply took her hand and pressed it to his skin once more.

She leaned back as she touched him tentatively and Benjamin steeled himself not to move, not to respond in kind. Sarah explored him carefully, her eyes widening as she took in the expanse of his chest. Benjamin caught his breath, his need for her growing stronger with every second. She inched her fingers down his abdomen, feeling the taut muscles.

"Wait, wait," he breathed, catching her hand and looking deeply into her eyes. "Sarah, I can't. We cannot… go further."

A raging war burst through him, his body screaming at him just to take her there and then while his mind insisted that he at least *try* to behave respectably.

"Why?" Her eyes were wide, her cheeks burning with heat. He did not want her to feel ashamed or embarrassed, did not want her to put the blame on herself.

"If you continue, then I will most likely take you to bed," Benjamin said, honestly. "Your touch sets me on fire even though you do not know it." He smiled softly and lifted his hand to brush back a tendril of hair from her face. "I am trying my best to do right by you." He could tell she was entirely innocent of all the goings on between man and woman and even that warned him away from continuing things.

"You are trying to be a respectable gentleman," Sarah

murmured, dropping her eyes from his. "I cannot fault you for that."

Benjamin wrapped one arm around her shoulders and held her close in an attempt to reassure her. "You have nothing to fear from me, Sarah. I want to continue this, truly I do, but I must know what I can offer you first."

She stiffened in his arms, her face turned away from him. "I will not prostitute myself, Lord Harrington."

He shook his head, upset that this was what she thought. "No, indeed, that was not what I meant." Catching her chin in his hand, he turned it gently until she looked at him. "This is all so very new to me, Sarah. I do not know what to do with such feelings, nor what they mean." Seeing her expression soften, he smiled gently. "Will you give me some time to work such things out? I promise I will not treat you any differently from how things have been before."

After a few moments, she nodded, no trace of anger or upset in her expression. Benjamin sighed heavily and held her in his arms, relaxing against the chair's back. "This is more difficult than I imagined," he muttered, wryly. "I had not thought that being respectable would be quite so trying."

Sarah laughed softly, resting her head against his shoulder. Benjamin smiled to himself as they sat there together, his heart growing warm with a sudden swell of peaceful happiness.

When he finally let her go, he gently did up the buttons on the back of her dress, issued a swift kiss on her brow, and sent her out the door as his manhood swelled in protest.

* * *

THE FOLLOWING MORNING, Benjamin tried to treat Sarah just as he normally would but found he simply could not prevent his eyes from straying toward her whenever he had a spare moment. Oftentimes he would discover that she was looking back at him, her eyes filled with something he could not quite understand.

It was both exciting and terrifying in equal measure.

Benjamin wanted her more today than he did yesterday, perhaps even more so knowing that he could not have her. He knew full well that his father would not take kindly to the news that he had taken one of the servants to bed, or that he'd chosen to make her his paramour. How strange it was to realize that the idea of suggesting such a thing to Sarah would be truly horrendous. She was worth more to him than just to be his occasional bed partner.

What was it that he was feeling for his servant? And *why* could he simply not remove her from his mind? She was worth her weight in pure gold given the amount of work she had done for him, but it was her compassionate heart and kind nature that continued to pull him closer. And, after what they had shared last evening, Benjamin couldn't ignore his longing for her.

But what kind of future can I offer her? he thought to himself, frowning. *She is a servant and I am of noble birth.*

But, then again, he was not the heir nor even the second son. Surely it would not matter whom he married?

Benjamin stared, unblinking, down at the paper in front of him. Marriage? When had he started considering that kind of idea? For almost as long as he could remember, the very notion had been distasteful to him, right up until he'd met Sarah. That was when things had begun to change, when he'd started considering things he'd never thought possible. Did he feel such for her because he was so far removed from his regular life?

However, in London there were women on every side who could make an appropriate wife and he had never thought the same of any of them. Besides that, there were plenty of comely maids about and he had not given them a second look.

Sarah. It was all because of Sarah. When he looked into her eyes, he wanted to be the respectable, honorable gentleman she could both trust and respect. In twining herself around his heart, she had forced him to consider his behavior and try to change it. All in all, she was good for him.

"Then perhaps Father will have no objection," Benjamin muttered to himself, his eyes darting to Sarah's small back once more. Could it be he had finally found a woman to settle down with?

CHAPTER 16

*S*ophie worked hard, refusing to allow her mind to wander. The fact that Lord Harrington was so close made things more difficult than usual, given what they'd shared last evening, but she was determined not to show him how much it had affected her. She would give him no cause to think she was slacking.

Yet, she could not stop herself from glancing over at him on occasion. Each time she did so, he was looking straight back at her, a strange smile on his lips. It was as if he could not quite work her out, as though she were a puzzle he could not solve.

Sophie too felt in something of a muddle. She had returned to her room last evening filled with a strong desire for… something. She could not explain the deep need beginning to surge within her, aware that her body was crying out, yet unsure of what that particular urge was. She had longed for more of Lord Harrington's kisses, and, despite her own misgivings, had allowed herself to explore his body further even when she knew she should be doing precisely the opposite.

She had been almost breathless as she'd touched him, fully aware that this was the first time she had done anything of the sort. Her mind had been trying to force her to be rational, but all coherent thought had left her as she'd traced her fingers over his bare skin. If he had not stopped her, she was not sure what would have happened. At the very least, she was aware of what went on between man and woman thanks to the crude words that had come from her cousin's mouth on more than one occasion, but she had never expected to feel such a strong desire for *more* of a man.

She realized how good it was of him to put a stop to things when he had the chance.

He had preserved her reputation and considered their future together — though what he thought that would look like, heaven only knew. It would all come crashing down anyway when he realized she had been lying to him. Of course, she could have taken the opportunity to explain to him the truth of who she was last night, but she had been so happy in his arms, so relaxed and at ease, that to ruin such a thing had seemed impossible.

The problem was that now, in the light of day, she was finding it more difficult than ever to even have a normal conversation with him. When he had come over to look at her work, her cheeks had warmed and her skin had rippled with an awareness of him. When he had placed a gentle hand on her shoulder, she had been forced to catch her breath. Trying and failing to talk normally, she had looked up at him and seen him smile, his gaze growing in intensity.

Had it not been for the the butler at the door, Sophie was quite sure he would have kissed her again.

At least the butler's presence had given her pause, reminding her that she was going to have to stay out of sight for the next few days if she did not want her cousin to discover her. She glanced up at Lord Harrington, seeing him frown at something on his desk. Should she now, perhaps, take the opportunity to share with him what it was she felt? Could she tell him about her cousin and beg him to forgive her for her deception? Surely he would understand when she told him everything that had happened. She took a breath.

"My lord?"

He looked up at her at once. "Yes, Sarah?"

"Might I speak to you for a moment?" she asked, quietly, her heart beating faster as she rose to her feet.

He nodded and grinned at her. "It is probably best that you stand on the opposite side of the desk from me." His eyes glittered and Sophie felt herself blush. She took her seat in one of the wingback chairs in front of him, her nerves causing anxiety to ripple through her frame. She knew what she had to do in telling him everything, but the truth was, she simply did not want to. It would take a great deal of courage and she had no idea what he might say once he discovered the truth.

"My lord," she began, "I– "

The door suddenly flew open and a familiar voice caught her ears.

"Ah, Harrington! The butler said I might find you here!"

Sophie scrambled from her seat, her heart thundering in her chest. She kept her back to her cousin, practically racing back to her desk, grateful she faced the wall. She felt sick, and it took everything within her to prevent her body from shaking uncontrollably.

"Dunstable!" Harrington boomed, getting up from his chair. "I had thought to expect you tomorrow!"

"Well, I found myself in the vicinity and thought why not just come here anyway? I have sent my servants back for my things. Is Haversham here yet?"

Lord Harrington chuckled. "He will be here this evening. Goodness, what a merry party we shall make!"

Seeing that they were both quite caught up in their reacquaintance, Sophie did the only thing she could think of and hurried from the room. She left the door ajar, hoping desperately that Lord Harrington would not call her back. Once free from the study, she ran the length of the hallway, fear chasing her all the way. Her cousin was here, and she had not had the time to tell Lord Harrington the truth.

* * *

"Oh, my dear!"

Mrs. Martins hurried toward her as Sophie made her way down the stairs, catching her hands and leading her into the kitchen. Mrs. Potts already had a hot toddy waiting for her, which Mrs. Martins pressed into her hands.

"He arrived unexpectedly," Mrs. Martins explained, quietly. "We did not know until he knocked on the door. I would have come to find you but he insisted on making his own way up to the study. He knows this house well, you see. He has visited here before when the family has been in residence."

Sophie lifted the hot toddy to her lips with trembling hands, the warm liquid burning down her throat as she sipped. Slowly, she felt a small amount of energy come back into her limbs, and she let out a long, shaky breath.

"I was about to tell Lord Harrington the truth of it all," Sophie mumbled, trying to calm her frantic mind. "But then my cousin walked in."

"Did he see you?" the cook asked, already back at the stove stirring something in preparation for the evening meal. "Did he know who you were?"

Sophie shook her head. "No, I am sure he did not. I kept my back to him and left immediately." She looked from one kind face to the next, her heart still pounding wildly. "What am I to do if Lord Harrington sends for me?"

Mrs. Martins paused for a moment, thinking carefully. "I doubt he will have his friends visit him in the study, for that is not often his practice. He will entertain them in the drawing room or dining room, even the library I suppose, but certainly not his study. You will be quite safe there, I should think."

Sophie swallowed the painful lump in her throat. "Perhaps you are right, but I still shall feel as though I am sitting on the edge of a precipice every time the door opens!"

The cook expression grew sympathetic. "Could you perhaps move your desk?"

She shook her head. "Not unless the master permitted it."

"You could ask him," Mrs. Martins suggested, tilting her head just a fraction. "I know you have been getting along rather well. He is not as offhand with you as he is with the rest of us, for whatever reason."

A river of heat climbed up Sophie's spine as she recalled how only just last evening she had been curled up in his arms.

"That's right!" Mrs. Potts exclaimed, her eyes brightening. "Make up some excuse and have him hide you in the corner of the room."

It was an idea at least. "It is already fairly alone in the corner of the room," Sophie murmured, her heart beginning to slow its painfully quick pace. "Do you know how long my cousin intends to stay?" She looked up at Mrs. Martins, who shook her head.

"These gentlemen do not seem to have a great deal of pressing matters to attend to," came the reply. "I do not know how long they will be with us. Usually, it is until they get somewhat bored or are required by their family to return home."

That did not bring much hope to Sophie's heart. "Then I shall have to endure in whatever way I can," she murmured, sinking into despair. "For I currently have nowhere else to go."

Mrs. Martins cleared her throat and put one hand on Sophie's arm. "Or you could continue with what you had always intended and tell him the truth," she reminded her, gently. "Take your rightful place as a lady of noble birth, and ask him to protect you. He will not refuse you, I am quite sure."

"But my cousin is his friend!" Sophie exclaimed, feeling more desperate than ever. "He might listen to me, but then discuss it with Malcolm. My cousin is more than able to convince him of his innocence and declare me quite mad which, given that I am dressed and working as a servant, might not seem such a far-flung idea. Malcolm is quite good at keeping up appearances. Even I did not see his true character for some time." She put her head in her hands, pressing the tears back from her eyes. "I do not know what to do," she finished, her voice by this time a breathy whisper.

There was a short silence, broken only by the sound of Mrs. Potts clattering about at the stove.

"Perhaps you need a little more faith in the master," Mrs. Martins said, eventually. "I have seen more of his good character these last few days than ever before. It may be something of a risk to speak to him so plainly, but he may come through for you. Think about it, Sophie."

Sophie sighed, not feeling even the slightest flicker of hope. "I will consider it," she promised, her angst not lessening in the least. "Thank you, Mrs. Martins."

CHAPTER 17

*F*or the next two days, Sophie continued as best she could, even though her nerves were so fraught that she could hardly do the equations she had once found so simple. To her great relief, she did not see Lord Harrington, nor Lord Haversham, and certainly not her cousin. At times, when she had been walking to the study, she had heard them talking and laughing together and she had practically flown down the corridor to avoid them.

She was constantly on her guard, fretting that she would be found — and found out. There was no opportunity for her to speak to Lord Harrington, although she was glad to hear, at least, that he was continuing to oversee the improvements to his tenant's homes. He had not allowed his friends' presence to push him from his tasks, even though he worked late and she early. In a way, Sophie was proud of him for sticking to his intentions, even though his friends certainly would be tempting him to do otherwise.

She also realized, with a sigh, that she missed him. She missed his teasing words, his wide smile, the spicy masculine smell of him working closely beside her, and the optimism he exuded about the world in general, with the exception of his own character.

She let herself into the study, seating herself at the desk where she had become quite comfortable over the past week. She had always been studious, and she enjoyed putting her intellect to good use in helping with matters of some importance.

She jumped when the door clicked open, and she whirled around to see who had entered, sighing when she saw it was Lord Harrington. She gave him a small smile as he made his way over to her.

"Busy working?" he asked, coming to stand beside her, his fingertips resting lightly on her shoulder, causing all of her senses to all leap to awareness.

"I am," she said, forcing herself to concentrate on his words. "I enjoy the work, to be honest. Thank you for all you have done for me."

He looked at her quizzically, his brows drawing together. "What do you mean?"

"For taking me in, and for allowing me to do this type of work," she said, before taking a deep breath. Now was the time to tell him to truth, to lay bare the who she was, the past, and the reason she was here.

"Lord– "

"Come," he interrupted, pulling her to her feet. "I must apologize for my lack of attentions and presence the past few days. With my friends' visit, I have been remiss."

"Not at all, my lord," she said, flustered at the close proximity of his hard chest at her nose. "There is nothing to apologize for. In fact, I should like to– "

He cut off her protests with a searing kiss, sending jolts of heat through her body as his mouth slanted over hers, his tongue stroking hers in a love play that made her weak. She melted into him, reveling in the warmth of his hard body.

She didn't want to give this up — give *him* up. He nibbled at her lip as he released her, before beginning to trail kisses down her neck.

"I'm happy to provide some distraction," he murmured, making her flush with delight. "I believe it's my turn to teach you something. I might struggle with accounts but I am proficient in many other things."

Sophie let her fingers pull him toward her as she rested her forehead against his. "I am quite happy to continue with the accounts, Lord Harrington, I assure you. Besides, there is a matter I wanted to discuss with you." She let her hands drop and carefully sat back down. He ran his hand through his hair, but allowed her to do as she wished.

"Ah, regarding the issue with the accounts," he said, shaking his head at her with a smile. "You are quite determined."

"Yes," Sophie said hesitatingly. "There is that."

His grin softened. "Do you think it ridiculous that I cannot do this myself — that I find such a simple thing so difficult?"

Sophie placed her hand on his, looking up at him earnestly. "No, not in the least."

Benjamin seemed to relax before her very eyes. "You are too good for me, Sarah." He held her gaze for a moment before clearing his throat. "Now, what do you say to a stroll in the garden?" He held up his hand when she began to protest. While her cousin was not likely to enter the study, there was a much greater chance she could encounter him in the garden. "I have a lovely little arbor where we might sit for a while and discuss all you would like to tell me."

The smile on his face was so endearing that Sophie knew she could not refuse without providing him proper explanation.

"Do you not think the rest of the household will find it strange for you to enter the arbor with a maid?" she asked.

"We shall be discreet," he said, which dampened her fears of running into Lord Dunstable. "Come, I know a way through the back of the gardens where no one will notice us."

"All right," she finally agreed, getting to her feet. "It sounds lovely, then."

"The French doors in the ballroom lead into a very pretty little patch and I am quite sure you will enjoy it."

"I should enjoy any time in your company, Lord Harrington," Sophie murmured as they walked to the door. "As much as I know I should not."

His eyes looked contemplative as he took in her words. "Do not concern yourself with that. Enjoy yourself for a few moments."

* * *

SOPHIE FELT a sense of peace as she leaned against the small wooden bench in the garden, taking in all the sights and sounds that surrounded her. While it could use more greenery, there were beautiful flowers, wonderful scents and birds of all kinds singing around them. It was like a little piece of heaven, made better by the proximity of the man with her.

Lord Harrington didn't sit next to her, but rather paced in front of her, seemingly unaffected by their surroundings. She supposed he was used to them.

"Lord Harrington," Sophie began.

"Benjamin."

She looked up at him. "Pardon me?"

"I feel as though you should call me Benjamin. Lord Harrington sounds too formal coming from your lips."

She inclined her head. "Very well. Benjamin."

"Sarah," he stopped his pacing as he turned to face her,

calling to her before she could begin. "I know you wanted to speak with me about the accounts, but for the moment I cannot truly concentrate on them. I must say something to you first."

She hoped he wasn't apologizing again. She didn't think she could take that anymore.

"I've told you that I am not a good man," he said, holding up a hand as she made to tell him otherwise. "Or if I am, as you seem to believe, then I have certainly done things contrary to that opinion. My father sent me here to this estate to learn responsibility, and also to take me far from London. My eyes were opened to the error of my ways before I left, but old habits are difficult to break. When I first saw you, I must admit that I instantly desired you — I hope that does not shock you. But I vowed to myself and to my father that I would not touch any of the staff.

"Then I came to know you. You, Sarah, are so good, so kind, so trustworthy. When I am around you, I want to be a better man. I do not care so much for the activities and the people I once seemed to hold so dear. I know what you will say. That you are a maid, not good enough for me. However it is quite the opposite. It is you that are too good for me. You see the very best in others, you are patient, you are understanding. And yet when I consider the time we have spent together I realize I have been as selfish as I always am. I have told you everything about me, but have asked nothing of you. I know only that your parents have passed and you have no siblings, but nothing further."

He walked to her, taking her hands in his.

"I want to know more, Sarah," he tilted her head up toward him.

She didn't want to ruin this moment, but what could she tell him? She turned to him, and looked up into his eyes, which burned with desire as he trailed a finger down her neck to her collarbone. "You're intelligent, I know that. But what else is there to you? What do you enjoy? What were you like as a child? What do you want of your life?"

She blinked. These were certainly not questions to ask a maid, but then, whatever was to become of them, they were far past the typical relationship between a maid and the lord of a manor.

"To answer your questions," she said slowly, "I enjoy reading. I love to lose myself in the stories of others. My— at one of my postings I was able to read from the massive library and it brought me much joy."

"My library is open to you, I hope you know that."

"Thank you, my lord."

"Benjamin."

"Thank you Benjamin. As a child, I was fairly quiet. I didn't get into much trouble, but I did love to hide myself away in pantries or a cabinets, and stay there for hours. My parents would look for me everywhere, and would finally find me engrossed in a novel."

She smiled in remembrance.

"And what do you want?"

She looked down at her hands. She had never truly thought much beyond escaping Malcolm.

"I suppose..." she started slowly, "I want a life of freedom, of purpose, of happiness. I want companionship. And love, if it's possible."

He nodded slowly, his gaze locking on hers.

"Benjamin— "

"Harrington!"

The voice, all too familiar and the cause of her nightmares, cut through the gardens. "Harrington, where have you buggered off to?"

"My apologies," Lord Harrington said remorsefully to

Sophie. "It seems Lord Dunstable is looking for me. I shall be but one moment."

He rose to greet his friend, slipping out of the arbor. Sophie, however, was taking no chances. The moment he was out of sight, she slipped out the other side and back to the relative safety of the house.

CHAPTER 18

*O*nce she had properly composed herself from the near meeting with Malcolm in the garden, Sophie spent the remainder of the day working in the study. Some hours later, she sat up, flexing her fingers, cramped from scribbling away at the accounts. She had taken a quick break for dinner and had then returned to the study to finish off writing her list of the remaining mistakes she had found in the ledger.

Glancing up at the clock, Sophie realized with a shock that it was much later than she had realized. Given that she was falling so far behind due to her nerves, Sophie had wanted to finish her task regardless of the time, knowing that Lords Harrington, Haversham, and Dunstable had all gone out for the evening.

However, it was now close to midnight. Sophie should have already been abed since she would have to wake up early to help with the morning duties. Closing the ledger and promising herself she would finish the task in the morning, she made for the door – only for it to open.

"I'm sure he keeps some brandy in here," she heard someone mutter and, with a gasp of fright, Sophie stepped back into the shadows. She pressed her hand to her mouth as her cousin stepped inside, swaying just a little. While Sophie had no wish to ever be in his presence, it was much worse when he was clearly deep in his cups, as he currently was. Fear clutched at her heart as she realized that he stood between her and the door. There was no way for her to escape. The night in the library of his home came rushing back to her, as did the fear she felt when he had chased her through the halls. She only had one choice — to hide.

Unfortunately, in her haste to sneak away to the dark corner of the room, she managed to trip over a footstool and went crashing to the ground with it.

"What the devil—?"

Sophie scrambled away, her ankle beginning to throb painfully. She tried to hide as best she could, but her cousin was already coming in search of her, his eyes piercing the darkness.

She screamed aloud as he reached forward and grabbed at her, his hands scrabbling in the darkness. "No, no!" she cried out, her heart beating so fast she thought she might be sick. "Leave me alone!"

"A pretty little maid, is it?" Lord Dunstable chuckled, using his strength to pull her against him, staggering back a little. "Come here, my sweet. I have been long missing the company of a warm body in my bed."

Sophie cried out and kicked him as hard as she could but found that she could not stand on her other leg at all. She collapsed on the ground as Lord Dunstable let out a cry of pain where she had connected, only for him then to grab her hair and attempt to haul her to her feet.

Recognition flared in his eyes when the light his her face.

"You little witch," Lord Dunstable hissed. He grabbed her face with one hand and pulled her closer to the candlelight. "Hiding away from me in the guise of a maid?"

"Leave me be!" Sophie whispered, struggling against him. "Leave me, I beg you!"

Lord Dunstable squeezed her cheeks painfully. "I have been searching high and low for you, and here you are in the home of my friend," he growled, pushing her against the wall so hard that all of her breath shot out of her body. "Did you really think you could hide from me forever?" He let his fingers trace down her throat, his other hand now on her arm. "I always get what I want, Sophie. You should know that by now."

Sophie cried out again, only to receive a sharp, stinging blow across the face. She tasted blood, her head spinning as she tried in vain to move away from him. Her ankle was too painful to stand on, and his strength was beginning to overcome her.

His hands began to rake at her skirts and, fighting with all she had, Sophie tried hard to push him away, screaming as loud as she could hoping someone — anyone — would hear her. He slapped her again but Sophie did not stop trying to wrench herself away from him. She tried to slump to the floor, but he grasped her shoulders and held her against the wall, pressing the length of his body against hers.

This was it. She was doomed. There was nothing she could do. Panic gripped her as he pressed his fingers to her throat, his meaning clear.

"Do not try to fight me anymore, Sophie," he whispered, threateningly. "I do not intend to make things easy for you. If you want to live, you will do just as I say."

"I'd rather die first," Sophie rasped out, hardly able to speak. "You shall never have me."

He chuckled, darkly. "We will see about that." He pressed his lips to hers and, even though she banged on his chest to try to make him let her go, he simply pushed himself against her all the more.

"What is the meaning of this?"

The door to the study flew open, slamming against the wall. Lord Dunstable stepped back from Sophie at once, and she slumped to the floor, drawing her knees up and letting her head fall into her arms as she tried to catch her breath.

"I'm just taking my pleasure with your maid," Lord Dunstable replied, with a touch of humor. "Nothing to see here, Harrington."

"It seems like she does not want your particular attentions, Dunstable," Harrington replied, firmly, stepping closer to Sophie. "And I do not want my staff treated in such a way."

Sophie shuddered violently and he bent down to look at her. He reached out a hand and lifted her head, horror filling his face when he saw her tear-stained cheeks and swollen face. Even though his touch on her cheek was gentle, she could not help but wince. Fury overcame him and a growl came from his throat turned sharply to the man.

She knew that now the truth would come out. Dunstable would not hide her identity. What would Harrington feel for her then, knowing she had lied to him for all this time?

"Get. Out."

Lord Harrington rose to his feet, glaring at Lord Dunstable, who merely laughed.

"I said, get out," Harrington repeated, glowering at him. "No one treats my staff this way. You are not welcome here, Dunstable."

"Ah, you feel something for the little maid," Lord Dunstable replied, easily. "If that is how you see her, I suppose she has not told you, then."

There was a short pause.

"Told me what?"

Lord Dunstable chuckled, wandering over to Sophie and reaching out a hand to her. As Sophie shuddered, Lord Harrington stepped between them, keeping Malcolm away.

"This is my fair cousin, Lord Harrington, the one I told you about — the one who went missing."

The atmosphere grew thick. Sophie could hardly breathe, desperate for Lord Harrington to understand.

"She belongs to me," Dunstable continued with a smug grin. "Miss Sophie Carmichael – her father was Lord Carmichael, although he died recently and she was left to my care."

"I am not yours," Sophie blurt out, her words shaky but with some strength. "I have rejected you again and again, why can you not leave me be?"

"Be silent!"

Lord Dunstable's words were like a gunshot, echoing through the room. Sophie shrank back, terrified that he would hurt her again.

"If she is your cousin," Harrington began, quietly, "then why did she end up in my phone, under some false pretense of being a servant?"

There was a short silence. Sophie, too afraid to say another word, prayed silently that Lord Harrington might take pity on her, might realize that her cousin was a tyrant, that she had been desperate to escape him.

"Because she is a foolhardy young thing who would not step in line," Lord Dunstable said, with a trace of anger lining his words. "Selfish, headstrong, and entirely willful."

"And it is not because she was running from you?" Lord Harrington continued, calmly. "Is what I walked in on how you treated her at home?"

Lord Dunstable chuckled. "She is mine to do with as I please."

Sophie's skin crawled with loathing and a prick of fear. If Lord Harrington turned his back on her now, then there would be nothing for her. She would end up as Lord Dunstable's plaything, never to have a life of her own.

Lifting her head, she looked up at Lord Harrington, who had turned toward her. His eyes flashed with emotion — of what, she wasn't sure. Silent tears continued to roll down her cheeks as Malcolm laughed.

"I think you ought to leave, Dunstable," Harrington said, eventually. He walked to the corner of the room and pulled at the bell multiple times, despite the hour.

Lord Dunstable snorted. "Very well, but I shall be taking my cousin with me."

"No," Lord Harrington interrupted, firmly. "You shall not. You'll never touch her again."

"I really do not think this has anything to do with you, Harrington," Lord Dunstable sneered at him as he walked over and grabbed Sophie by the wrist. "I apologize my cousin wormed her way into your home. We shall be going now."

"You will go alone," Lord Harrington stalked over to them, gripping Dunstable's arm until he let go of Sophie, and she shifted as far away from Malcolm as she could. "And I do have a say. She is to be my wife."

There was a pause, only for Lord Dunstable to start laughing incredulously. "Sophie?" he cried, mockingly. "*You* intend to marry *her*? Do not make me laugh so!"

Sophie, who was similarly aghast, although for different reasons, gazed up at Lord Harrington. He did not look at her, but grasped Lord Dunstable by the collar with strong hands and lifted him, bodily, away from Sophie.

"I said, get out," he breathed, his voice dangerously low. "You are not welcome here. Stay away from me and away from her You will never touch her again."

"You will regret this, Harrington," Dunstable exclaimed, his expression altogether ugly.

"Never," Lord Harrington replied, opening the door to his study and practically throwing Lord Dunstable out. "I regret only bringing you here. Now get out and go home. I never want to see you in my house again."

CHAPTER 19

*B*enjamin did not know what to do with the anger rushing through his veins as Dunstable glared at him through the open doorway, a sneering expression on his face as he carefully straightened his shirt.

"She's mine, Harrington."

Benjamin's fingers slowly curled into fists as he stepped forward. "Get out of here, Dunstable. She'll never belong to you."

"You're a fool," Dunstable mocked, his lip curling. "A soft-hearted, stupid, fool."

Glancing along the corridor to see two slightly weary-looking footmen approaching, Benjamin smiled darkly and stepped closer. "If you don't leave my house this minute, I'll have you thrown out. Never return, Dunstable, if you don't want your actions on the lips of the biggest gossips of the *ton*."

Dunstable's eyes narrowed and, for a moment, Benjamin thought he might raise his hand at him, but instead he stepped away from Benjamin and began to walk down the hall. Benjamin watched him for a moment, his back straight and his fists clenched.

"Lord Dunstable is leaving us," he said to one of the footmen. "Have his carriage called and ensure he is packed and gone within the hour. Rouse the cook and have her send up a tray for Miss Carmichael." He saw the flicker of confusion on the footman's face but did not explain. "I will need some cool compresses, food, and hot tea. And then inform the butler that the house is to rise two hours later than usual. There will be no need for an early breakfast."

The footmen, who had clearly been sleeping and had risen on hearing the bell, looked both pleased and relieved.

"Right away, my lord," one of them murmured, and together they walked after Lord Dunstable.

Benjamin, relieved that he did not need to concern himself with Lord Dunstable any longer, allowed his fury to cool for a moment longer before returning to the study. His eyes searched the room for Sarah – Sophie – only to find her huddled in a corner, her hands over her eyes.

His body was rife with emotions. The anger still simmered within him, and his stomach twisted when he thought of what Dunstable had done — and what he had tried to do. But why had she lied to him, hidden in his home as a maid? He was baffled. That question, however, would have to wait.

"Come," he murmured, hurrying toward her, helping lift her to her feet. "You need to sit by the fire."

Sophie dropped her hands but winced as she tried to put weight on her foot. "I am terribly sorry for all that I have done," she said quietly, unable to look at him. "I will leave your house at once."

Benjamin shook his head, firmly. "None of that," he promised, bending to scoop her up into his arms. "Now, if you will permit me."

He heard Sophie gasp as he lifted her, and he realized just how light she was. His eyes took in her swollen face, his anger beginning to burn in his belly once more. Carefully, he carried her toward the chairs by the fire and, setting her down gently, he bent down to push her hair out of her face. She jerked away from him, and he cringed at the reaction, but after a moment she moved back toward his touch. He persisted with gentle motions until, finally, he could see her face in its entirety.

He tried to keep his rage toward Dunstable from rising to the surface again as he took in the marks on her face. He felt sick that he had caused this to happen.

"Why did you not tell me?" he rasped.

Her eyes finally rose to meet his, although they continued to dart away now and again.

"I am sorry, my lord, I tried—"

"You should have told me before I invited the man into my home," he said rising, angry now that he had brought the very man that she was running from to his house for his own mere amusement. "In fact, you should have told me the moment you arrived. I would have provided you what you had needed, rather than making you work as a servant in my house."

Bloody hell, he had done exactly what he had come here to avoid — take after a young woman, desire her, act on it, steal kisses and nearly more while she had been here hiding from a man just like him.

"You were afraid of me," he said quietly, realizing her reason for keeping silent. "You were afraid I was like your cousin. Perhaps you were right. Perhaps I am not so different. I chased after you, attempting drunken kisses and to undress you by the fire."

"You are *not* like him at all," she cut in with vehemence. "I knew from the start you were not like him. I saw good in your character. I saw that you had the desire, the *need* to change into the man you wanted to become."

"The man my father wants me to be, else I shall lose my inheritance," Benjamin added, but Sophie shook her head.

"No," she stated, with a degree of firmness he was not expecting. "I saw that you wanted to change your ways for your own self. You looked back at your past with regret, not with delight. That was why I wanted to speak to you, to tell you the truth about who I was and why I had made myself a servant in your home."

"And yet you did not say anything," he said, "despite the fact we sat in here together, day after day."

"I could just never find the words," she said, looking at him with eyes begging him to accept her explanation and apology. "And I tried, truly I did, multiple times, but we were always interrupted or another matter arose."

He knew, however, it was more than that. She may say she thought he was a changed man, but somewhere, niggling in the back of her mind, he was sure she was concerned that he was the same sort of man as her cousin — a man who would take what he wanted without thinking of how his actions might affect her. And was he truly that different from Dunstable? Benjamin had left London for nearly similar reasons to what he had done here with her. If word got out that Sophie had been in his home for days now, spending solitary time with him, closed in his study at all hours of the night, she would surely be ruined.

He sighed. "Tell me how you came to be here," he said, taking the seat across from her, noticing as he did how she flinched when he walked by her.

Sophie nodded, closing her eyes for a moment as pain crossed her face. "He was so persistent," she said as she opened her eyes, her expression blank. "I managed to hide in my room and I wore the only key to the door around my neck, but the servants told me he intended to bring in a blacksmith so that I should have no escape." She swallowed and looked away.

"Malcolm's cook, she was kind to me," Sophie continued as a shudder ran through her. "She made arrangements with her sister, Mrs. Potts, for me to escape and find my way here. If she had not, then I might now be – "

"Do not think of it," Benjamin replied, firmly, hating that she was so shaken. He gently caught her hands and, much to his relief, she did not pull away. Instead, she drew in one long, shaky breath, letting it out again slowly as her trembling began to diminish. "You are quite safe now, Sophie," he continued, softly. "I meant every word I said to Dunstable."

"Thank you, my lord," she replied, staring down into the fire that was beginning to wan. "However, I will not hold you to the promises you made."

"I— I will marry you, if you so wish it," he said, hating that he stuttered over his intention. "I will not ruin yet another woman."

Her eyes flew up to meet his.

"You … you ruined someone?"

He felt the heat creeping up his neck as he realized he had said more than he meant to. "I've told you, Sar– Sophie, I'm not the most reputable man. The rumors you have heard are true. You should know this before agreeing to marriage with me."

"Why do you want to marry me?" she asked, as if she had not heard his previous words.

"Why?" he asked. "Because you are a young woman who has spent a week living in the home of a man who is known for his rakish ways, who has nearly ruined women before. Because you need protection from Dunstable. I am only the third son of a duke, but a duke nonetheless. I would be a good match for you."

"That is all?"

"That is more than enough reason!" he exclaimed.

She nodded but said nothing.

"I believe I should retire for the night," she finally said, after a silence stretched between them. "It has been a trying evening."

"Of course," he nodded, and walked over to help her but she shrank back from him. He gave her the space she required as she limped past him to the door.

"Goodnight, my lord."

"It's Benjamin, Sophie, remember?"

She nodded, then stepped into the hall, quietly shutting the door behind her. He didn't know what to make of the woman. She was typically quiet and demure, and yet possessed an inner strength and a will of steel. She would not bend to the desires of others, and still knew how to treat all with kindness. She was willing to see past the faults of most people to the goodness within.

She had been through so much in the past. He wanted to do right by her, he truly did. Though he had seen the way she looked at him, the way she retreated from him when he came too near. Perhaps she would never truly want him. Was he ready for this — or marriage? He cared for her, yet knew so little about her.

He sighed as he stood, ringing the bell for Mrs. Martins. The woman arrived in her nightclothes and wrapper, brushing sleep from her eyes. When he explained what had happened and that Sophie required some attention, Mrs. Martins came awake at once.

"Of course, I shall go to her immediately, my lord," she exclaimed. "You say Lord Dunstable is gone?"

"Yes, he's been escorted out by the footmen," he said with a nod. "If only I had known…"

He looked at the woman, who had her head bowed.

"Were you aware of this, Mrs. Martins?"

"I— yes, I am afraid I was, my lord."

"And you did not think to inform me?" he crossed his arms over his chest.

"My lord... Lord Dunstable, he's an earl, and I am a housekeeper. I would not like to make accusations against one of his stature."

Benjamin began to pace the room. Did all his staff think him in the same company of such a man, that he would over-look Dunstable's actions?

"In the future, Mrs. Martins," he bit out as he walked circles in the carpet before coming to stand in front of the bewildered housekeeper. "You will keep me informed of anything you may know of guests who have been invited to my home. In addition, should the staff require anything for their comfort or safety, you will come to me with it. Now, please see to Sophie. I assume you know her true identity, as all but me seem to be aware of the goings on of this house-hold. Dunstable left some marks on her that need attending to. And, if you would, move her to a guest chamber."

The woman said nothing, but nodded at him with wide eyes and left nearly as quickly as Sophie had.

Benjamin moved to the sideboard and poured himself a good measure of brandy. He took a sip, staring into the contents of his glass, then frowned at himself. Old habits were hard to dismiss. Resolving that this would be his one and only drink of the evening, he sat down heavily in his chair in front of the fire and contemplated what to do now.

He had told Dunstable he would marry Sophie in order to force the man to leave. He had then told her he would follow through to save her reputation. He put a hand to his face. Yes, he wanted her, but did he want *marriage* to her? He had thought so, but she seemed frightened of him, as despite his best efforts he had proven to be the man they had all thought him to be. The rake who took women as he wished, preferring the company of friends who turned out to be less than savory characters. He thought back to Miss Simons, the woman he had nearly ruined in London. Did she see him as Sophie did Dunstable?

He sighed and decided that come morning he would speak to Sophie and determine what she wanted. He would go through with this marriage if she so wished, but if not, he would consider how best to help her. He thought of the pretty smile and joy he had seen in the wide hazel eyes during the hours she had spent in his study, and the way they had darkened when she had wanted him the night in front of the fire. That a man like Dunstable, a man he had brought into his home, should dim the spirit within her, make her into the timid, spooked creature she was tonight, made his heart ache.

He would do right by her, in whatever way she wished. It was the least he could do.

CHAPTER 20

When Sophie woke, the first thing she felt was panic. She had overslept and there were duties to perform and accounts to review and—

Pulling back the linen bedsheets, Sophie swung her legs around, only to discover that she was no longer in her servant's room, nor her small, uncomfortable bed, but rather the large, beautifully decorated bedroom that Mrs. Martins had led her to last evening. Floral patterns adorned the wall-paper and carpet, the draperies of the bed a dusky pink.

She also realized that her ankle was still aching.

Relief coursed through her veins as she pulled herself back into bed, drawing the covers up to her chin and settling her head back on the pillow. Warmth began to seep back into her limbs as she lay there, the niggling of fear still creeping in, but she told herself to crush it. For the first time in years, she should have faith that she was truly safe.

She had nothing to fear any longer. There was no one coming to try and take something from her that she did not want to give. There was no threat of violence. She was no longer alone.

She thought of Lord Harrington's words the night before. If she so chose, she could be his wife. He had offered his hand to her freely. She frowned, however, as she thought of the reasons he had provided to her. He would marry her to protect her reputation as well as her body from Dunstable.

It was for better reasons than many married, but is this what she truly wanted? Now that she had come to know him, the man he truly was, she wanted more than that from him. She wanted him to marry her because he cared for her, because he couldn't live without her. She wanted his love, she realized with a start, as she became aware of the depth of her own feeling toward him. She loved him.

When he had rushed into the study last night, she had felt a crushing relief. She trusted in him, knew he would protect her. Despite what he said of himself, she saw the man he was, the man he was growing to be. He was a man who saw the good in a person, who had simply needed a purpose to keep himself from throwing his life away.

He was all she could have asked for. If she chose, he could be her family, her protector, and her lover. That brought a rush of heat to her core, and Sophie did not deny that the thought of being in his arms again was a most welcome one. Was it to be, however? Should she hold him to his promise of marriage, or let him go?

She knew she wasn't worthy of him. He was the son of a duke, and she the daughter of a mere viscount, who had acted as his maid, for goodness sake. He was marrying her out of a sense of duty, to prove to himself and his father that he was not the man he once was. That was not the basis of the marriage she now wanted with him. She might have depths of emotion for him, but enough that she did not want to tie him to her if he did not feel the same. But if she were not to stay with him... where else was she to go?

She would have to make her way to London, and find a

position as a governess, or perhaps a bookkeeper. She had a few funds which would allow her to journey there and she would have to quickly locate a place of work. For all that she could plan though, in her heart she did not want to leave.

Sophie sighed and determined she would think on this more in a few hours. For now, she would appreciate the safety she felt in this bed, in this home. Snuggling into her covers a little more, Sophie allowed herself to drift back into sleep.

* * *

SOME HOURS LATER, Sophie rose and dressed, choosing to breakfast in her room. The maid who attended stared wide eyed at her for a moment, embarrassing Sophie. Of course, she had worked alongside these girls for some time, only now to reveal that she was, in fact, a lady.

"I do apologize for my deception," she murmured, as the maid set down the breakfast tray. "I hid my true self only because it was necessary, I assure you."

"Oh, we bear you no ill will, Sarah – I mean, Miss Carmichael," the maid said, blushing furiously at her mistake. "The master spoke to Mrs. Martins and then Mrs. Martins told us everything. We understand why you had to do what you did."

Sophie managed a smile. "I am relieved to hear it, I must say. And it is Sophie."

The maid smiled back at her. "Everyone knows you're a good-hearted soul and, from what Mrs. Martins says, you've been through some trying times. We're all so glad for you, Miss Carmichael, truly." She bobbed a quick curtsy before leaving the room as Sophie smiled after her. The staff had forgiven her already, it seemed. Mrs. Martins would have been careful in what she said, Sophie was quite sure.

Finishing her warm chocolate, Sophie got to her feet and brushed down her skirts, feeling more than ready for the day.

The fact that Malcolm was gone from the house was an overwhelming feeling, as was the fact that the staff seemed to have forgiven her and she no longer had to pretend to be someone she was not. All that was left was to determine what to do about Lord Harrington's proposition.

Opening the door to her bedroom, Sophie paused to straighten the embroidered white shawl around her shoulders before making her way to the study. Her leg did not hurt half as much as before and, so long as she took care, her wrapped ankle did not protest too much when she put weight on it.

Sophie was determined to put herself to some useful endeavor, if nothing else, to show her gratefulness. She did not want to neglect the accounts, not when she knew Benjamin found them somewhat difficult, and she was so close to finishing her review. Besides which, she had not spoken to him of the mistakes she had found, although she was now quite certain that they were not simply accidental.

On finding no one within the study, Sophie carefully made her way to her desk in the corner of the room, sat down, and began to continue with her work.

"Sophie!"

Glancing up, her quill pausing in its work, Sophie could not help but laugh at the astonished expression on Benjamin's face.

"Whatever is the matter?" she asked, as he came over and took the quill from her hand before pulling her up to stand next to him.

He shook his head, his gaze unreadable. "You do not need to do the accounts any longer," he said quietly, his hands going around her waist to help her away from the desk. "You do not work for me anymore. You never *should* have been working for me."

"I really do not mind," she said, "it's the least I can do…"

"Sophie," he stopped her. "We must speak of your – our – future."

She nodded and stood, finding herself quite close to him, feeling the heat through his linen shirt. She looked up, and her face came just inches away from his. She licked her lips as her pulse began racing.

"You don't shrink from me today," he commented.

"No," she responded, bowing her head. "My apologies. Last night I was… I couldn't help but…"

"I understand," he said. "A man such as me is not so different than Lord Dunstable. I should have realized how you would feel."

"That is not it at all!" she exclaimed. "You would not press unwanted attentions on me—"

"But I did. I went so far I caused you to slap me."

"And you stopped," she said. "That would have only redoubled the efforts of my cousin."

He looked down at her and reached down to cup her cheek. "I am so very sorry for what you have been through."

He began to speak, but Sophie tilted her head to him and pressed her mouth against his gently. When he groaned, she could not help but melt against him, her arms going around his neck almost of their own accord. She lost herself when she was with him. She forgot to worry about the future, where she would go, what she would do, and that she would be alone once more.

The heat from his body burned her, setting her alight as he angled his head. His hand reached between them, cupping her breast, stroking her through the thin fabric of her dress. She gave a soft moan, and his hands slid behind her, cupping her backside as he lifted her up on the desk against his stirring manhood, that longed to—

He pushed away from her, breathing heavily.

"Bloody hell," he cursed as Sophie tried to slow her pulse.

"Whatever is the matter?" she asked breathily, her fingers still twined around his lapels.

"After everything you've been through, I cannot keep my hands off you for one day," he muttered in disgust. "I suppose it proves I am the man everyone believes me to be."

"Was I not the one to press my attentions on you?" she asked, raising her eyebrows.

He shook his head. "Well, at the very least, I suppose I cannot ruin you, as we are now betrothed."

She angled her head as she looked up at him. "And that is why you feel you should marry me, to save me from ruination?"

"Did we not already discuss this last night?" he said in frustration. "Of course! I told my father I would show him I am not the man he thought. It seems he was correct in his assumptions, but the least I can do is prove to him that now I will take responsibility for my actions."

Her eyes fell to the floor before they snapped up to meet his.

"I shall be no one's responsibility, *my lord*," she said, anger in her voice.

"What do you mean?" he asked, the bite in her tone apparently surprising him.

"I *mean* that I do not wish to be a burden, or to owe anyone anything. I apologize for using your home as a safe haven. You did not ask for my deception, but I did not ask for marriage. I will not have you take me as a bride out of misplaced guilt over kisses in the study. My reputation does not matter to me, but rather that I am free from my cousin.

You have allowed that to be so, and I thank you for that. But please, do not worry yourself about me any longer."

She moved to walk past him, and he reached out to grab her arm.

"Sophie—"

"Don't touch me!" she said, jumping away from him, reacting without thinking before seeing the shock and dismay on his face. "I am sorry, I didn't mean—"

"No need to explain. I understand," he said, turning his face away from her. "Go if that's what you want. I'll contact my father and have him arrange a place for you in the city, where you will be safe. Go to the parlor if you'd be more comfortable there."

Tears sprang into her eyes and she watched him as he took his seat in the chair behind his desk. He looked confused, and it tugged at her heart, but she refused to allow herself to give into her emotions. He felt a responsibility toward her and obviously desire, but not love or even affection anymore, which is what she needed. She turned and left the room, her skirts but a whisper as she walked out the door.

CHAPTER 21

*C*oward, she said to herself as she packed her bag with her few belongings. Why could she not voice what she truly wanted to Benjamin?

Because she was afraid of his response. A man like him had been with many women — beautiful, experienced women. She was sure he had his choice of many potential brides in London. She would not tie him down to her out of a sense of obligation.

She sat down at the desk in her room and penned a few quick notes, to Mrs. Martins, Mrs. Potts, and Benjamin himself. They were short thank yous, for allowing her reprieve from her cousin, providing her with a refuge. She apologized for any deception and asked for forgiveness.

She moved stealthily through the house to avoid notice. She knew if anyone saw her they would urge her to stay, but she would be a burden to no one any longer. She had enough coin that if she could find a way to London, she could lose herself in the city, where she could put herself up for a few nights at an inn before seeking out employment. Perhaps she would be better off as a governess, she thought. She had proved somewhat adapt at teaching Benjamin his figures, and she wasn't sure she could pass herself off as a maid again without someone like Mrs. Martins to help her.

It took some time, but she convinced the groom to help her prepare her horse. She told him she was simply meeting a family member at the nearby inn. Perhaps there she could sell her horse and find passage to London. She felt a stab of guilt at her lie. It seemed all of the staff was aware by now of her true identity, and the groom saw no reason not to believe her.

As she rode away from the property, tears began to stream down Sophie's face as she thought of Benjamin. Would he feel relief to be freed from his promise to her? Would he be angry that she had left without a word? She had not known him long, but already she realized just how much she would miss him.

The longer she stayed, however, the more her feelings for him would grow and the harder it would be to leave. She had not said goodbye because a few soft words or kisses from him and she would be lost to his charm, and a burden once more.

She had not ridden far when she heard the rumble of a carriage approaching from behind her. She tried to make her way off the road unseen, but it quickly rounded the curve behind her before she could hide.

"Sophie!" she heard the voice through the carriage doors as it pulled to a stop beside her. Had Benjamin realized she had left already? How could he have known so soon?

Frowning as the carriage pulled up next to her, she could not see the person within. Sophie thought that Benjamin had sounded a little different from before.

A tingle of unease coursed through her as she began to urge her horse away, but she was too late.

A strong hand shot out from within as Malcolm burst

from the carriage. Her horse backed away quickly, but Malcolm held onto the reins and pulled her down quickly. Before she knew it, a knife was pressed against her throat. Sophie tried to scream but the blade pressed a little harder against her skin, forcing her to remain quiet.

"Don't even think about it, Sophie," Malcolm hissed, his voice sending shivers of terror straight through her. "Did you really think that I'd just do as your lover said and leave without you?" He chuckled mirthlessly, making her shudder. "I've told you more than once that I always get what I want – and that includes you."

"Please," Sophie managed to whisper, her heart thudding painfully in her chest. "Just leave me alone!"

His grip tightened painfully. "Never," he bit out, harshly. "You're mine and no one else's. And my dear Sophie, how easy you made this for me! Now walk!"

Sophie had no other choice but to move away from her horse as Malcolm released the knife from her throat but now pressed it against her back. It was do what he said or risk losing her life.

"And if you scream or try to run, I'll cut you into pieces," Malcolm said, firmly, as they got to his own carriage. "I'd rather have you dead than in his arms."

Hearing the coldness of his words, Sophie knew that he would do exactly that. He had gone quite mad with rage and she was forced to do as he asked. Despair began to build as she tried to stall in front of the the enclosed carriage that would carry her away with the man she had tried so hard to escape from. Why had she been so stupid as to leave Benjamin's home?

"Get in," Malcolm said, pushing her forward. "And remember, not a sound."

Stumbling slightly, Sophie managed to climb into the carriage, wincing as her ankle began to throb once more.

The carriage moved almost at once, taking her away from the only safety she had known since she had left her cousin's home. Her heart ached. Benjamin would read her note and believe she had left of her own will. He would never know she had been taken. How could she possibly rid herself of her cousin now?

* * *

BENJAMIN ROSE when he heard a knock on the study door. "Come in," he said, looking up, hopeful to find Sophie at his door, but instead he found Mrs. Martins standing there, looking at him nervously as she folded a piece of vellum in her hands.

"Mrs. Martins," he said, rising. Guilt pricked at him for how he had spoken to her last night. Clearly he had somewhat terrified the woman, although he had thought her a stoic sort. "Can I help you?"

"My lord..." her voice trailed. "It seems Miss Carmichael has... left."

"She what?"

"She left, my lord," she replied, her eyes flicking from one side of the room to the other but never landing on him. "She left me a note, and there was one with your name on it as well."

She walked over to him, passing him the sheet of paper with somewhat tremulous fingers. He was shocked to find his fingers shaking as well as he opened the paper, though from nerves or anger, he wasn't sure. He didn't even notice Mrs. Martins quietly leaving the room, closing the door behind her.

The note was not long, written in the elegant handwriting he had begun to know so well.

Dear Lord Harrington,

Thank you for all you have done for me. I have felt nothing but your kindness and generosity in my time as both a maid and a guest in your home. I appreciate all you have offered me but I find that I am unable to accept. I no longer wish to be a burden to you or your family.

I have finally found the courage to do what I should have from the beginning — find a place for myself, where no one knows me or my background, far from my cousin and all he has threatened.

I wish you well. Know you are a good man, and I hope you find the love and happiness you deserve.

Yours always,
Sophie

Benjamin's fist closed over the paper, wrinkling it in his palm. She was gone. She wished him well. A growl escaped his throat as he thought of her alone on the road. He told himself the ache that began to throb in his chest was due to his worry for her unprotected state, and not because of what he felt for her.

He knew he wanted her, that much was certain. And he cared for her. What he felt for her ran much deeper than any feelings he had held for other women before, who he wanted for their bodies and not who they truly were on the inside.

It was his own fault that she had left. With his kisses and

taking advantage, he had pushed her away. She didn't want to be tied to marriage to a man like him, and could no longer abide to be under the same roof. His gaze drifted over to the seat where she had bent over her work for so many days. Her ink and quill sat waiting for her return. His anger boiling to the surface, he strode over and threw them to the floor. Breathing heavily, he marched to the sideboard and poured himself a good-sized drink from the decanter. As he threw it back swiftly, it burned his throat, settling in the pit of his stomach, where it simmered in the emptiness that remained.

* * *

HE WAS SITTING THERE in his chair, a second drink in, when a knock came on the door and his butler entered.

"My lord," he began, "Lord Haversham is in the drawing room, questioning your absence as well as that of Lord Dunstable. Do you wish me to—"

"Bloody hell," he interrupted. "I completely forgot the man. I'll see to him myself."

If he was going to drink, he might as well not drink alone. Besides that, he realized he had entirely neglected to tell Haversham what had been going on with Dunstable. He had been too caught up with Sophie's situation. However, Lord Haversham must now be quite confused as to what had happened to his companions.

Benjamin found him standing in the drawing room, drink in hand, looking most perturbed.

"My apologies, Haversham," Benjamin said as he walked in. "In truth – and you must not take this badly – I quite forgot about you."

The man did not look the least bit offended, although his pale blue eyes registered a little surprise.

"Lord Dunstable has been removed from my house,"

Benjamin continued, quickly explaining what had taken place last night. "I am sorry to say that his time here has come to an abrupt end although, of course, you are more than welcome to remain."

Lord Haversham frowned, rubbing one hand over his brow. He appeared quite dazed and Benjamin wondered if the man was still suffering the ill effects of drinking a little too much brandy the previous evening.

"Lord Dunstable went last night, you say?" Lord Haversham muttered, looking thoroughly confused. "I must say, that does not seem quite right."

Benjamin bit back a sigh and cleared his throat instead, drawing Haversham's attention. "What do you mean, Haversham?"

"I mean that I was quite sure I saw Lord Dunstable outside my window this morning."

An icy hand of fear wrapped itself around Benjamin's heart. "Outside your window?"

"Yes, I'm quite sure it was him," Lord Haversham continued, still frowning. "I thought it odd he was in his carriage around the back of the house. I couldn't understand it, to be quite honest with you. Then his carriage took off as I left my room and looked out. It seemed to be in quite the hurry."

Benjamin did not wait to hear another word, his heart slamming wildly into his chest as he hurried from the room, practically running through the halls, shouting for his housekeeper.

"Mrs. Martins!" he called frantically. "Mrs. Martins!"

The woman stepped out of the servants' quarters, a shocked look on her face.

"When did she leave — Sophie?" he asked, his gaze wild.

"I found the notes on my desk just minutes ago, so it could have been any time this morning. Perhaps the grooms will know," she said. "Why, is something the matter?"

"I believe Lord Dunstable may have followed her," he said. "I must go after her at once."

Benjamin drew in a deep breath, steadying himself for a moment. He had no thought but for Sophie, his heart crying out for her already. He knew if Dunstable had her, he would not give her back without a fight. He couldn't think of what might have happened to her already.

Running full tilt, Benjamin raced to the stables, shouting wildly for his horse. The groomsmen, although startled to see him in such a wild state, did as they were bid and, within minutes, Benjamin was mounting his horse – a large, black stallion he knew to be a fast ride. He had no weapon with him but could not risk returning for one, aware that every moment that passed was another moment that Sophie was going farther and farther away from him.

Benjamin was thankful that the ground was damp, and he was able to make out the carriage tracks clearly. His heart pounded in fear as he rode, terrified that Dunstable had already done something to Sophie. Berating himself as he pushed his horse faster, Benjamin cursed himself under his breath for leaving their conversation on bad terms, for not being more attentive to the fact that Lord Dunstable might have meant every word he said, every threat he'd made. Benjamin had been foolish enough to believe that Dunstable had simply turned back for home, as though Benjamin's warnings had forced the man to quietly leave without trying to reclaim what he considered to be his.

"I will find you, Sophie," Benjamin whispered into the wind as he pushed his horse to a gallop. "I swear I will find you."

CHAPTER 22

A sudden shriek rent the air, and Benjamin reined his horse in, making it rear up. Managing to keep his seat, he held on tightly, forcing his stallion to remain still. He could hear shouts, mingled with cries of fright which tore at his heart. It had to be Sophie.

Dismounting, he quickly tied his horse to a nearby tree and, making his way slowly forward, saw the carriage up ahead, just around the corner. The canopy of trees made it a gloomy patch of earth, adding to his anxiety. He could hear the sounds of a flowing river coming from somewhere close by, though he could not quite make out where it was coming from. Pressing himself against a large tree trunk, he carefully looked around it to get a closer look at the carriage.

Sophie was standing in the door of the carriage, one hand pressed to her neck. Blood seeped out between her fingers and Benjamin felt himself go cold with fear.

"Drop it," he heard Dunstable snarl, seeing the man standing outside the carriage. "You don't have the strength, Sophie."

Benjamin moved closer, his feet barely making a sound of

the soft grass. His stomach tightened in worry as he saw Sophie holding a long, silver knife in her other hand. It was shaking so badly that he wondered if she would be able to hold onto it for much longer, although it was the only thing between her and Lord Dunstable. She looked to be weakening by the second, clearly in a lot of pain from the knife wound to her neck.

Without thinking, he strode forward, his eyes focused on Lord Dunstable.

"Ho!" he roared, seeing Dunstable jump in surprise. "Get away from her, Dunstable!"

"Harrington," Dunstable sneered, not moving an inch. "How unsurprising. Of course, you're aware that I expected you to follow us."

"But you did not expect Sophie to manage to display such strength as this and hold you back from your destination," Benjamin replied, hurrying forward as fast as he could manage. "Although I will tear you limb from limb if you have hurt her." His jaw clenched as he drew closer, seeing the redness of the blood in stark contrast to her pale skin.

Without warning, Dunstable lunged forward and hit Sophie's arm, hard. She cried out and dropped the knife, stumbling back so that she fell into the carriage. Dunstable made to pick up the weapon but, without even thinking, Benjamin rushed forward and slammed himself into Dunstable. The man stumbled forward, while Benjamin struggled to regain his balance. The knife lay, glinting on the earth just behind him and Benjamin lunged for it, only for a fist to come flying into his face. Stunned, he stumbled back before falling over completely. His heart thundered in his chest as he tried to right himself, horrified that Dunstable might have retrieved his knife.

"Stop!"

Sophie's shout echoed through the trees, sending crows

flying from the branches in fright. Still a little dazed, Benjamin shook his head to clear his vision before getting to his feet, seeing Sophie standing, knife in hand, directly in front of Dunstable.

"I will never, *never*, go with you," she said to at him, her voice loud and firm. "I am tired of being treated as though I am your plaything."

Dunstable made to say something but Sophie took a step forward, her hand steady now as she held the knife out toward him. "Enough, cousin. I am finished with this." She glanced down at the knife, before returning her gaze to Dunstable. Benjamin finally made it to her side, his breath coming in short, sharp gasps.

"I am finished with all of this," she said, a little more quietly. "You will never have me, Dunstable. This is over."

And, so saying, she flung the knife as far away as she could. It was not a perfect throw by any means, but it was far enough that it disappeared over the edge of the path, down to where the river flowed. At the same time, Dunstable let out a scream of rage and looked, for one moment, as if he might launch himself at Sophie. Benjamin stepped in front of her, his free hand finding her own cold one and holding onto it as though it were his only lifeline.

"Go, Dunstable," he growled, his brows furrowing. "Sophie is not to be yours. You have lost. Go, or it will be all the worse for you."

Slowly, he began to back away, taking Sophie with him. Dunstable's face was, by this time, a deep red, and Benjamin could not be sure what it was he intended to do. He could take no risks, could not turn his back on him.

"Go to my horse," he muttered to Sophie. "Go now. Quickly. It is just around the corner."

She left him, hurrying away, and Benjamin saw Dunstable's eyes follow her along the path. The evil gleam within them frightened Benjamin more than he would ever admit. It was as though the man was possessed, gone mad over what he could not have.

The moment Dunstable ran for him, Benjamin was ready. He ran forward to meet his charge, ducked under Dunstable's right arm as it came out to greet him and pummelled the man full in the ribs. Dunstable cried out and staggered back, but Benjamin did not wait for him to get his bearings. With two hard blows, he had Dunstable lying on the ground, unconscious. The man had been too desperate in his attack, too hasty and careless.

Benjamin put his hands on his knees and drew in three long breaths, calming himself as well as ensuring that Dunstable was, truly, knocked out. There was no movement other than the slow rise and fall of the man's chest and so, no longer afraid that he might attack him again, Benjamin turned to look for Sophie, finding her not at his horse but rather with her own mare a short distance away, watching him.

She looked so weary his heart ached for her. Her eyes were tired, her neck stained with blood. She was resting against her horse who, to her credit, was standing tall and strong, as if realizing her lady needed her.

"Sophie," he called, running toward her. "Oh, Sophie."

The moment he reached her, she clung to him as though they had been parted for a great many days. Her hands wound around his neck, her face pressed into his shoulder and Benjamin could do nothing but hold her tightly. Sobs racked her body, the shock of what had occurred taking over. Wanting to ease her suffering, Benjamin whispered comforting words into her hair, rubbing her back gently.

"How badly did he hurt you?" he asked, stepping back and looking down at the cut to her neck. It was not a particularly deep cut but it had bled badly. The sight of it sparked fury in his veins, making him wish that he had thrown the man, face down, into the river. "I should– "

"Take me home, Benjamin."

Sophie's beseeching cry had caused his heart to rend into pieces. His anger died away like a doused candle flame and, in a moment, he had her up on his stallion.

Lord Haversham, accompanied by his groomsmen, rounded the corner in that moment, and he gratefully welcomed the man, who looked quite shocked as he took in the scene. Haversham promised to see to Dunstable and one of his groomsmen would bring Sophie's mare home.

"Your cousin will not return to hurt you," Benjamin promised Sophie, before pulling himself up behind her and leaving his friend to deal with the mess. He wanted only to concern himself with Sophie, who sat proud on his horse, despite all that she had gone through.

He said nothing else, but pulled her head back against his chest. He knew she didn't want him, didn't love him, but he vowed to do all he could to protect her in the future. Not because he had to, but because he wanted to. He cared for her. He had never experienced such feelings before, but as they blossomed in his chest and he held her tight against him, he realized with a shock what he felt for her. He loved her. He loved her gentle spirit, her compassion, her willingness to overlook all of his flaws and find the good in him.

He didn't want to scare her by pouring out the words to her now, overwhelming her after all she had been through. He settled for wrapping an arm tightly around her, as he set the horse to return home.

"Oh, Benjamin," she whispered, finally sagging back against him as weakness took over her body. She did not say another word and Benjamin held her tightly as they rode back, the love he had for her washing all through him until he could think of nothing else.

* * *

Sᴏᴘʜɪᴇ ᴄʟᴜɴɢ to Benjamin as he led her inside, her body still slightly shaking. Benjamin shouted orders left and right, scooping her up to carry her upstairs to her room, despite her protests, with apparently great ease.

She was tired. So tired. Weak, from all that had happened and in pain from the bruises and cuts Dunstable had inflicted on her. But yet, despite all of this, Sophie knew she was safe. She was back home. There was nothing to worry her, nothing to make her afraid for her life. She was with Benjamin and that meant safety.

The staff who had eyed her warily on her first day now did everything possible to help her, as they had come to accept her. Sophie saw Mrs. Martins directing maids here and there in her room, giving her fresh sheets on the bed, soft towels warming by the fire and the promise that a bath was being drawn for her. Sophie made to protest but, as Benjamin set her down carefully in a chair by the fire, he shook his head, and pressed her hand gently.

"Trust me, luv," he whispered, gently. "You need this. Mrs. Martins will see to the wound on your neck and will decide if you need a doctor."

"You are not leaving me?" Sophie said at once, clasping his fingers tightly. "Don't leave me, Benjamin."

She knew it was not her place to ask, after all that she had put him through, all he had done for her already. But she wanted nothing more than for him to take her in his arms and show her that everything would be all right.

Something flashed in his eyes, although his gaze softened. "As much as I would like to stay, I cannot," he said, softly, the corner of his mouth lifting. "I do not think Mrs. Martins would think it at all proper during your bath."

Sophie flushed, loosening her grip on Benjamin's hand.

"No, I suppose you cannot. But, Benjamin, please…. please, don't go far."

"I will be back the moment you are ready to receive me," he promised, leaning forward to brush his lips against her forehead. She closed her eyes, realizing she had no desire to pull back from his kiss. "I have some correspondence to see to, but it will not take me long. You will be quite safe here, with Mrs. Martins."

"I know," Sophie whispered, hating that he had to leave her side, even for a short time. "Thank you, Benjamin."

His smile seemed forced as his gaze drifted to her neck and then back up to her eyes. "You have shown more strength than I would have ever expected," he said, softly. "I am terribly proud of you."

Sophie closed her eyes to stop tears from slipping down her cheeks. She wanted him more than she could ever dream. When she had seen him come round the corner, her heart had felt full to bursting at the relief that coursed through her and the love she felt for him. He squeezed her hand gently once more, before his footsteps made their way past her chair and toward the door. She heard him say something to Mrs. Martins before the door closed tightly.

"There, now," Mrs. Martins murmured, coming over toward Sophie. "You have been through a great ordeal, have you not? How glad I am that you are all right!" She gently tipped Sophie's head to one side, hissing through her teeth at the sight of the mark on Sophie's neck. "Goodness, but he cut you badly. It stretches almost from your collarbone to your jaw!"

"It is not too painful now," Sophie replied, wondering if the shock of it all had, somehow, lessened the discomfort. "He was going to take me to the deepest part of the woodland, so I knew I had to act." Talking through what had happened did not bring her any additional pain, recounting it as though she were merely an outsider who had watched the entire thing unfold.

"He clenched the knife tightly and, as I tried to grasp it, he sliced his arm upwards. I tried to dodge out of the way but the carriage was small and so it caught my skin." Sophie closed her eyes, not quite sure what had happened next. "I think I must have knocked him from the carriage as I fell, trying to avoid the knife, for the next thing I knew he was on the ground outside and the knife was on the floor of the carriage."

Mrs. Martins put one gentle hand on Sophie's shoulder, her face lined with both anxiety and sympathy. "You are incredibly brave, my dear."

"Not really," Sophie replied, her voice growing hoarse. "I had no other choice. I could not allow him just to use me as he pleased. I had to try to defend myself."

"And the master came just as you were doing so?"

Sophie nodded, relief covering her like a warm blanket. "I'm very grateful. If he had not come when he did... "

Mrs. Martins smiled, even though her eyes were sparkling with tears. "Do not think of it, dear. You will be a wonderful mistress in this house, I am quite sure." She sniffed once, wiped at her eyes, and smiled.

"Oh no," said Sophie, her eyes wide. "I must still speak to Lord Harrington, but I do not think—"

"None of that now," Mrs. Martins cut her off, in a much brisker tone. "You should have seen the man, first when he found you had left and then when he determined you may still be in danger from Lord Dunstable. I've never seen him in such a state. Now, If you'll just come this way, dear. The bath should be prepared for you now."

Sophie managed a wobbly smile in return and rose to her feet, following Mrs. Martins from her bedchamber into a smaller room where there was a steaming bathtub waiting for her. Scents of lavender and rose filled her nostrils, helping her to slowly relax. There was a warm fire in the grate and a screen in the corner.

"I have a maid here to help you undress and wash your hair," Mrs. Martins continued, as she shut the door behind them both. "I'll take your things straight away to be washed."

Sophie smiled gratefully. "Thank you, Mrs. Martins."

The housekeeper returned her smile, her expression gentle. "You are most welcome, Miss Sophie. Welcome home."

CHAPTER 23

Two hours later, Sophie was washed, dried, and dressed in a night rail and wrapper. She had chosen to sit by the fire with a tea tray in front of her. Mrs. Martins had examined the cut to her neck and had determined it did not need stitching, although she had given Sophie a medicinal salve with which to place on it to aid its healing. Sophie had done as instructed, wrinkling her nose at the smell, but had to admit that, already, the ache was lessening.

"Thank you, Mrs. Martins," she murmured, as the woman made her way to the bedroom door. "You have been very good to me."

"It is no more than you deserve," the housekeeper replied, smiling. "Now, I am quite sure the master will wish to see you." Her eyes flickered over Sophie. "Are you ready to see him?"

Pulling her wrapper a little tighter, Sophie nodded, aware that it was quite untoward to let a gentleman into her room when she was in such a state of dress, but found that she did not care. Her reputation was rather ruined as it was, and she would prefer to take a few moments alone with him than be concerned of what people may think. After what they had been through together, she wished for nothing more than his company.

"Let me go in search of him," Mrs. Martins replied with a smile, before closing the door.

Sophie let out a breath, her stomach rolling with unexpected butterflies as Mrs. Martins left the room. Now that the shock of what had happened had begun to wear off, she was scared of the strength of her attachment to Benjamin. Her desire for him, for his company and for his love, had grown to such depths that she was afraid to give in entirely to what she felt, not quite certain where it would lead.

* * *

"Sophie?"

Benjamin took a hesitant step through the doorway, before hurrying toward her and dropping to his knees in front of where she sat in the corner chair, so that he might look up into her face.

"I am fine, I assure you," Sophie whispered, her hand tracing his features gently. "Thank you, Benjamin, for all that you have done. I'm sorry—"

"Enough of that," he said, though he softened his words with a wide hand spanned across her cheek. "I proposed marriage to you before because I could not imagine sending you back to him and it was the only way to keep you safe. I still want to marry you, but not only for those reasons."

She blinked once, twice, before managing a tremulous smile. "I have hidden so much from you," she murmured. "How can you forgive me after what I have done?"

"Because I know why you did it," Benjamin replied, an ache in his throat as he saw just how vulnerable she truly was. "You had to escape your cousin and you had no one to turn to."

"I did not know your character, else I would have told you all from the beginning."

Benjamin shook his head. "I can understand your thoughts toward me. I did not treat you with the respect you deserved, but only made you think I was just like Dunstable."

Revulsion and anger swirled within him once more as he thought of the man he had once considered a friend. "You– you've changed me, Sophie. I want to show you the man I am, the man I know I can be. You must know I am not like your cousin. I…" he stopped and took her hands in his. "Miss Sophie Carmichael, will you be my wife? I can think of no other who will do me so well as you. With you by my side, I will not stray. My course will be straight, my life a responsible one."

Sophie swallowed, no smile on her face. She studied him for a long moment, her eyes contemplative. "I do not think I am worthy of you, my lord," she said, eventually. "I can bring nothing but trouble to you. My cousin –"

"Will no longer be an issue. I will never let him hurt you," Benjamin interrupted, quickly. "Do not think of him. You will bring me a great deal of good, Sophie, I know it," he finished, not understanding why her gaze was still so closed off and unsure.

As she looked down at him with wanting, waiting eyes, the love bloomed in his chest and he finally recognized what she was waiting for. What a fool he had been. What she wanted to know was the depths of his heart. "I cannot deny that I hold a deep affection for you."

Her breath caught and her eyes widened as she looked back at him.

"You make me a better man, but it's more than that. Whether you are a lady or a maid, I care naught. What I care about is the love I have for you and what you may feel for me," Benjamin promised, his own heart beating fast as he placed his emotions before her. There was no pain, no embarrassment in being so open and so vulnerable, only a wondrous, freeing feeling that grew with every word he spoke.

"You love me?" Her expression was incredulous, her eyes burning with an inner fire as if she could hardly believe the words.

"I do," he answered, softly. "I love you, Sophie Carmichael. I cannot imagine being without you. I only ask that you forgive me for how I have acted toward you these past weeks."

Her face broke into a grin, and her smile was radiant, despite the pain that she obviously still felt from her ordeal. "Benjamin," she said, his name on her lips causing a stirring within him. "There is absolutely nothing to apologize for. I *welcomed* your kisses. In fact, I want nothing but more of them. I thought you were marrying me out of duty, and I had no wish for you to tie me to you as a burden for the rest of your life."

"Never a burden," he said, relief washing over him that she did not fear him, nor think of him as the facade of a man he had been.

"Benjamin Harrington, I would be love nothing more than to be your bride. I believe I have long felt the same, although I have been terribly confused."

"Then it shall confuse you no longer," he breathed, joy lifting his heart. "My dear Sophie, I shall make you my wife just as soon as I am able." He kissed her gently, refusing to allow himself to plumb the depths of his feelings toward her as he reminded himself of what she had just gone through. Stars seemed to sparkle around her as he drew back, her wide hazel eyes full of love as she looked at him. She meant more to him than he thought anyone ever could. "You are a remarkable woman," he finally said, softly. "I cannot believe all that you have endured. I know you have been alone for a long time and I promise you that you will never be alone again. In fact," he laughed, "you may regret the people around you once you meet my family!"

Tears began to run down her cheeks in earnest. Benjamin pulled a handkerchief from his pocket, carefully wiping them away. He smiled at her gently as he took her hand once more, hating that her lovely face was marred by the marks of her cousin.

He reached for her then, and she came willingly. His kiss was slow and soft, as he did not want to hurry her. Sophie buried her hands in his hair and leaned down a little more, angling her head. He jerked in surprise at her boldness as she nipped at his bottom lip but, in a moment, his hands were around her waist and he was pulling her to the edge of the chair, his chest pressed to hers.

* * *

"Sophie," he gasped, breaking the kiss and looking into her eyes. "We shouldn't continue. Not until we are wed. I swore to myself I wouldn't take you before then."

"You love me, do you not?" Sophie whispered, refusing to release him.

"I do," came his breathless reply.

"Then you have nothing to fear," she replied. "I do not know what it is to experience love between man and woman but I do know I want to share it with you." She felt no shame or embarrassment at saying such a thing, her heart bursting with love for him, secure in the knowledge that he felt the same for her.

He groaned aloud and rested his forehead against hers for

a moment, his hands still spanning her waist. "You're much too tempting," he whispered before his mouth found hers once more.

Sophie, wanting to prove to him just how much she needed him, how much she wanted him now in this moment, managed to get to her feet, her fingers tearing at her wrapper. She shook with both nerves and heightened desire as she allowed it to pool on the floor. His eyes glittered as he watched her, making it almost too difficult for her to breathe. Sophie closed her eyes as he gently reached for the hem of her dress, moving carefully so as not to bring her any more pain. He gradually brought it over her head, and her skin tingled with the awareness of being entirely bare before his heated gaze. Her heart thumped wildly and she swallowed hard, finally bringing her eyes to his.

Suddenly embarrassed by her nakedness, she moved her arms to cover herself but he gently held them at her side. "No," he murmured. "Let me see you."

She let her arms drop before finally bringing her eyes up to his. What she saw was complete and utter shock, followed by a hungry desire that, much to her surprise, matched her own. Sophie shuddered, putting one hand out to rest on his shoulder, suddenly weak with all that she felt.

"You are utterly exquisite," Benjamin breathed, reaching out one hand to run his fingers lightly along her arm. "I can hardly believe that you are mine."

CHAPTER 24

*B*enjamin could hardly speak with the beauty lying before him. Sophie's hands straying to cover herself, but he caught them both before she could do so, standing up next to her. Then, stepping back from her, he allowed his gaze to glide over her form, his desire growing with each moment.

"If we go forward now, I won't be able to stop," he said, his voice nearly a whisper as he held her hands in his. "Tell me now."

Her eyes met his, burning with a passion he had not expected to see. "I trust you, Benjamin. I love you. Please, I – I want this, whatever it is…" She trailed off, looking a little uncertain as though unable to explain what it was coursing through her.

Benjamin well understood what she wanted, the ache beginning to burn deep within his own core. He could wait no longer.

Pulling her into his embrace, he kissed her, hard, remembering just in time to be careful of her wound. Sophie did not hold back, her fingers tangling in his hair as she deepened the kiss, surprising him once again. He ran his hands over her body, delighting in all the sensations that ran through him. Slowly, he walked her toward the bed, never breaking their connection.

"Wait," he said, his voice hoarse as she began to unbutton his shirt, vividly recalling just how she had touched him there only a few nights before. He smiled as she raised her hands and gently pushed away his fingers. She caught her lip between those endearing slightly crooked teeth as she concentrated on undoing the buttons. Never had a woman undressing him put him so on edge. Much to his own surprise, he felt a little embarrassed as she stripped him of his clothing, aware of just how intently she watched him. Her gasp made him smile when he finally stood naked before her, seeing the mounting blush in her cheeks.

"Come here, love," he crooned, wanting to ease the clear bewilderment she felt from what he could only assume was the first man she had ever seen wholly naked. "Let me kiss you again."

To his delight, she went willingly, lying back on the bed as he climbed over her, pressing his body against hers. His every sense burst to life, so aware he was of where their skin touched. He broke their kiss to look down into her face, her eyes lidded, her mouth slightly swollen from his constant attentions. Her breasts molded against his chest as he pressed against her belly and his need for her grew ever stronger. Her breath was quickening, her body growing taut beneath him as he lowered his mouth to hers again.

The truth was, Benjamin had never experienced anything like this. He had, of course, taken a number of women to his bed, but never one for whom he held any sort of emotion. Somehow, it intensified the experience, making it bigger and brighter than ever before. Every touch, every kiss, every breath was intoxicating.

Moving slowly down her body, Benjamin began to plant delicate kisses along her collarbone, a soft moan escaping her lips. Carefully, he gently cupped one of her breasts, remembering that this was her first experience of love, and carefully brushed her nipples. Sophie shivered beneath him, her breath quickening all the more as he lowered his head toward them, pressing his mouth to her skin until, finally, it covered her nipple. Sophie arched her back so forcefully that she almost came off the bed, and, in his surprise, Benjamin stopped what he was doing at once, afraid he had hurt her.

"What are you doing?" Sophie asked, her eyes wide and skin burning with heat.

"I – I'm sorry, I – "

"Don't stop now!" she exclaimed, flopping back onto the bed and reaching for him. Her fingers caught his hair and brought his head back to where he had been. "Please don't stop, Benjamin."

A small chuckle escaped him as he began his exploration of her body once more, delighted with how she'd responded to him. She was more passionate than he had ever expected or could have asked for. Slowly continuing his way down, Benjamin ran his hands down her thighs, slowly bringing them back up the inside of her legs. She groaned aloud as his lips replaced his hands, and he trailed kisses on the inside of her thighs before she allowed him to press his fingers against her core.

She let out a soft cry as he began to stroke her, fighting to keep his own desire for her under control. Normally, he was a somewhat-selfish lover. He would help women reach their fulfillment, but he primarily took for himself, looking for his own pleasures. With her, it was different. This was with Sophie, the woman he loved. Her innocence was her gift to him and he was going to accept it with both gratefulness and consideration.

"Don't fight it," he murmured, seeing her eyes flutter closed as he pressed one gentle finger into her. "Just allow it to happen, Sophie. It's nothing to be afraid of."

He did not have to wait long. Her entire body began to strain as she neared her climax, and, with a loud cry, she began to tense around his fingers. Biting his lip, he waited for her release to ebb, thinking to himself that he would never fail to recall this moment. The way she looked now, entirely, beautifully, exposed, was something he would never forget.

"Here, now," he said, moving back up to her head and brushing a kiss against her lips. "There will be pain, but only for a moment. I promise you."

She smiled up at him, her eyes swimming with a myriad of emotions. "Make me yours, Benjamin," she whispered, wrapping her arms around his neck. "I want only you."

He did not have to be invited twice. His arousal dipped into her, but he hesitated as it met her barrier. "One moment, love, and it will all be well again," he said before pushing forward.

She clenched around him, her eyes squeezing shut before, slowly, she began to relax. Benjamin forced himself to hold still, waiting for her pain to ebb away. When she looked up at him, her expression clear, he began to move within her once more, keeping his strokes slow and languid, waiting for her breathing to quicken again before making love to her in earnest. Her tight core made his blood run hot, his body burning from within. He lost all awareness of everything else, focused on the woman he loved, the only one he desired.

It wasn't long before he felt the heat within him rising to a peak. Benjamin pressed himself into her one last time, his mind telling him to pull himself from her before it was too late.

Sophie kept her hands around his neck, her eyes fixed on

his as she gasped in pleasure. He had no need to leave her. She was to be his, forever. With a loud cry of his own, Benjamin stilled, his body shuddering as he reached his fulfilment, aware that this was the first time he had ever spilled himself into a woman. He had no regrets.

After a few moments, Benjamin lay down beside her, pulling Sophie into his arms and brushing his lips against her temple.

"I am yours now," he murmured in her ear, "and you are mine. We are twined together now, as one."

"As one," she repeated a soft smile on her face. "Oh, Benjamin, I do love you."

"And I love you," he replied, his words honest and true, filling him with happiness and contentment. His eyes slid closed as she rested against him, his body growing tired as he lay there with her. He had never felt more at peace in his life.

* * *

SOPHIE ROSE the following morning alone in her bed, though she could make out the wrinkles in the sheets where Benjamin had spent the previous night. She smiled at the joy that filled her heart when she thought of him and their future.

After dressing, she lazily made her way downstairs to the dining room, passing Mrs. Martins on the way, who gave her a loving smile, causing Sophie to return it.

As she knew him to typically be a late riser, she was shocked to find Benjamin waiting for her at the table. He stood with a wide grin as she entered, pulling out a chair for her to sit close to him.

Unaffected by the servants around them, he brushed her forehead with his lips. "Good morning, love. I must tell you, our dishonest steward has now been sent away from the property, and Haversham has also taken his leave following yesterday's events. He wishes you farewell. I have also written to my father and mother and invited them to come to the estate straightaway. We shall require witnesses for our wedding and they will do very nicely."

A swirl of anxiety rippled through Sophie's stomach and her smile faltered as the repercussions of what he said broke through her cloud of happiness. "I am glad to hear the man will no longer be an issue. Benjamin, do you think your parents will like me? After all I have done? All I hid from you?"

Benjamin paused with his coffee cup halfway to his lips, his expression turning solemn. "After they hear all about what you have done for me, and what you have endured, I know they will love you as I do," he replied, quietly, his dark eyes blazing into her. "You have been the greatest influence on my life, helping me to take my responsibilities seriously and focusing on what is truly important. I look back on my past with shame but my future is now shining brightly, so long as I have you by my side."

Sophie felt her nerves settle again, reassured by his words. "Then I very much look forward to meeting them," she replied, quietly. "I hope I shall make you proud."

His eyes practically glowed as he took both her hands in his own. "You already do," he murmured, tenderly. "I know how fortunate I am to have you in my life. You need have no fear about my parents nor our future. It will be happier than you have ever known." Dropping a quick kiss on the back of her hands, he smiled into her eyes. "Come now, you must be hungry."

She smiled as she poured herself a cup of tea and buttered her toast. So much had happened that she still felt she was walking in some kind of dream, sure to wake up at any moment. Yet she knew it was true. She was to be Benjamin's wife and be safe, forever, from her cousin. Not only that, but their union would be one of love and affection, not simply out of necessity or obligation. That made it even more wondrous to her.

* * *

"AND MAY I PRESENT SOPHIE — my fiancée," Benjamin grinned, as Sophie curtsied beautifully, her cheeks pink as his father and mother rushed to greet her.

His father, normally quite nonchalant, took Sophie's hand in one of his own and patted the back of her hand with the other.

"May I say just how delighted I am to have you as a daughter-in-law," he said, firmly, throwing a glance toward Benjamin.

"We are not wed yet, father," Benjamin reminded him, with a chuckle, "soon, though."

"And we shall be glad to witness it," his mother replied, fervently, taking Sophie's arm and leading her to sit down on the Louis XV sofa together. "Now, tell me what on earth has happened with this cousin of yours?"

Sophie looked up at Benjamin, not quite sure what to say. Her fingers gently touched the spot on her neck that was still healing, although, after a week of ointments and the like, it was doing much better.

"I am not quite sure where he is," she replied, seeing Benjamin's nod. "I have had a few threatening letters but nothing concrete."

"I tried not to let her see the letters," Benjamin interjected, seeing the look his mother threw his way. "She was determined."

His father cleared his throat. "Well, you will be glad to know that I was able to assist you as you requested. I believe that the man shall not dare even come near you ever again!"

"Good," Benjamin replied, stepping forward to shake his father's hand firmly. "That is very good, Father. I thank you."

Sophie cleared her throat, looking up at Benjamin inquisitively. "What is it that you have done, Benjamin?"

He grinned. "I did not tell you, not until I was certain all had worked out as it has, but Father has helped me secure a lot of shares in the companies your cousin involves himself in. I did need help with some of the accounting," he continued, with a rueful grin, "but all is in order. Should your cousin come near us or threaten you again, then Father and I will be quick to throw those companies into disarray if we must – which will mean financial ruin for him."

Sophie's mouth rounded as she stared at him, "Why Benjamin, that's brilliant. You would truly do this for my sake?" she asked, her gaze going to his father before returning to Benjamin. "I can hardly believe it."

"Believe it!" his father exclaimed with a chuckle. "You are to be family now, Sophie, and we Harringtons take care of our own. After what you did to help Benjamin with the accounts and to uncover a very untrustworthy steward, I must say I think you a wonderful asset to our family." Benjamin saw his father share a knowing look with his mother, wondering what it was his father had yet to say.

"Your father and I have come up with an idea," his mother added, patting Sophie's hand. "One that I think will bring you both a great deal of joy."

"Indeed," his father replied, with a quick smile. "I must say, I am truly impressed with the change in you, Benjamin. I thought you quite lost for a while, I will admit."

Benjamin chuckled, a wry smile on his lips. "And lost I might well still be if it were not for this woman," he answered, softly. "Sophie has done me a world of good."

"Then I hope you will be very happy here," his father replied, smiling. "Benjamin, I am giving you and Sophie this estate as your own. Do with it as you wish, although I am quite certain that, with Sophie by your side, you shall not see it fail."

Benjamin did not know what to say, astonishment rippling through him. "You are giving me this?" he repeated, looking over at Sophie, who looked as surprised as he felt.

"Indeed we are," his father chuckled, slapping him on the back. "You have made me proud, son. I am glad that you have found yourself a good woman to be your wife. Strive only to be worthy of her."

"I intend to," Benjamin replied, quietly, seeing the blossoming smile on Sophie's face as she realized that this estate was now to be their home. "Thank you, Father."

"Thank you," Sophie repeated, a single tear slipping from her eye onto her cheek. "Truly, I am so very grateful."

"We will leave you for a moment," his mother replied, rising to her feet and excusing herself from the room, taking her husband with her.

Benjamin smiled and came to take the seat next to Sophie, holding her hands tightly between his. "Are you quite all right, love?"

"I am," she breathed, her eyes filled with wonder. "It is all just so much to take in. I have gone from having no family of my own to having one who cares for me just as blood kin might do. It's actually a bit overwhelming."

He smiled, running one finger lightly down her cheek. "And overwhelmed you will be, with my mother in your life," he laughed before growing serious. "But you deserve to be treated this way, Sophie. You are a beautiful, kind, and gentle spirit who brings such light and such happiness into my home and into my heart. I cannot wait to start our lives here together. I know that with you by my side, we shall have a very happy home."

"I can never thank you enough for all you have done for me," she whispered, settling one arm around his neck. "But I promise I shall do my utmost to show you in the years that follow."

"I do not want your thanks but only your love," he replied.

Her expression softened, her mouth growing close to his. "You already have it," she whispered, before kissing him once more.

EPILOGUE

*S*ophie sat at the table, silent as she basked in the warmth of the chatter around her, the smiles the siblings bestowed on one another, and the animation in her husband's eyes as he bantered with his sister.

"Do you know what I think?" Polly leaned over and hissed to Benjamin, "I think Thomas is a pirate now!"

"Do not be a nitwit, Polly," he responded to his sister, rolling his eyes. "Thomas? The man has spent his life living by the rules."

"I think Eleanor's changed him. Look at him, Ben! His face simply glows."

"Because of the sun, Polly," he said, sighing.

"I know I'm right," she said, dismissing him and sitting back in her chair smugly.

"Shush," said Benjamin's sister Violet, as she tried to temper Polly's enthusiasm. Sophie caught the raise of Eleanor's eyebrow as she seemed to have heard them, but she said nothing, though a small smile curled at her lips.

Thomas and Eleanor had returned for Sophie and Benjamin's wedding, and now they celebrated with a wedding breakfast. Sophie had chosen an emerald-green dress for the occasion, one which complimented her pale skin and her cheeks, which were stained crimson all day from the attentions of her husband and the happiness at their union. They had been officially married quickly after the scandal with the Earl of Dunstable, but they had a second wedding, one with Benjamin's entire family, a couple of months later.

"It is such a relief that the whole horrid affair with that despicable man is behind us," said Marie with an exaggerated sigh. "While I should never want to speak ill of the dead, we may all rest easier knowing that dear Sophie is now safe from that horrid man!"

"Mama," Violet said, sending her a look. "The man was Sophie's cousin."

"It's all right," Sophie interjected. "He was horrid."

Soon after Lord Haversham had delivered Lord Dunstable back to his home, Benjamin and his brother Daniel had paid a visit to the man, letting him know that Sophie was now under the protection of the family and any further threats to her were a threat to all of the Duke of Ware's kin and he would be best to stay far, far away. They explained the threat of financial ruin if he were to come near. They heard nothing more from him until a few weeks later, when Sophie had been shocked to receive word he had been killed from a fall off his horse. Benjamin had said nothing, though Sophie didn't miss the speculative looked that had crossed his face.

Benjamin was worried that Sophie would be over-whelmed by the whole of them, but far from it. Sophie reveled in their warmth and was so grateful to be part of such a family.

"I must apologize, my dear," Benjamin's mother, Marie, said addressing her. "These children of mine..." she sighed.

"Well, I've done my best, but I've never been able to manage them."

"There is certainly nothing to apologize for," she said with a smile at the dignified older woman, still beautiful despite the wrinkles of worry her children had given her and the dark hair that was graying at the temples. "This is all I could have ever asked for and more."

Marie gave her a secret smile. "In truth, I would not ask for anything different. But please, do not tell any of them that. Now, tell me, when can I expect a grandchild from you?"

Sophie's mouth gaped open for a moment at the woman's forwardness.

"Enough, Mama," Benjamin cut in, leaning over Sophie to give his mother a look. "It was simply months ago you were pressing for me to marry. You must be content with that for a moment, at least."

"Very well," she said, her gaze circling the table until they alighted on her eldest son, who was busy shoving food into his mouth to try to keep from having to answer the questions his youngest sister, Polly, threw his way. "Daniel! Do you see how happy a wife has made your brother?"

Benjamin gave a bark of laughter, and whispered to Sophie, "She'll never change."

As Sophie smiled at him, he picked up her hand and kissed the back of it. "She's right, however. You do make me happy, and have given me purpose to life. I've found my way, who I truly am."

"And yet your spirit hasn't changed," she said, smiling softly, her heart swelling with joy. "I believe that is what I love most about you. You have become more to me than I ever thought possible."

He rubbed the palm of her hand with his thumb and index finger.

"What do you say we leave this wedding breakfast and have a celebration of our own, just the two of us?" he leaned in and whispered in her ear.

"I believe your mother would be quite upset," Sophie said, though a tingle ran through her as the breath of his whisper kissed her ear. "In due time, darling. We have all the time in the world."

"Yes," he said with a wicked grin, "and I know exactly how to use it. By showing you just how much I love you."

THE END

* * *

Dear reader,

Thank you for reading Benjamin and Sophie's story! I hope you enjoyed their across-class romance and unexpected love.

Benjamin's sister, Polly, has grown up over the last three Searching Hearts books, and is ready to find her own happily ever after. You can find her story in book 4 in the series, which also features a familiar face from Clue of Affection, book 2 from the series. Read on for a preview of the story of Polly and her protector — or find your copy here: Hope of Romance.

If you haven't yet signed up for my newsletter, I would love to have you join us! You will receive a free book, as well as links to giveaways, sales, new releases, and stories about my coffee addiction, my struggle to keep my plants alive, and how much trouble one loveable wolf-lookalike dog can get into.

Until next time, happy reading!

* * *

Hope of Romance
Searching Hearts Book 4

A hopeless romantic. A jaded protector. A love that knows no bounds.

Following the marriages of three of her siblings, Polly Harrington can hardly wait to have a Season of her own in the hopes of finding the romance she's always dreamt of. When the Earl of Yardley charms her with good looks and attentions, she ignores all warnings to stay away.

After losing his heart years ago, Lord Sebastian Taylor is determined to never marry again. Instead, he spends his time on his estate and assisting the constabulary with cases involving the nobility. When he learns of Lord Yardley's scheme to ruin a young woman of the ton, he cannot stand idly by.

As he sets out to protect Lady Polly, Sebastian tries to deny his growing attraction to her, while Polly is confused by her feelings toward the stubborn man. Can they see beyond past hurts and their differences to find happiness with one another?

AN EXCERPT FROM HOPE OF ROMANCE

"*O*h, Polly, I have some simply marvelous news for you!"

"Just a moment, Mama," Polly murmured, setting her paintbrush carefully to the canvas. Her mother clicked her tongue rather impatiently, but Polly was not about to be put off. She had spent most of the long winter months trying to steadily improve her painting and drawing, and this piece was to be the culmination of those efforts.

She twisted her head and closed one eye to get a better look at the subject in front of her. Unfortunately, that subject had other ideas. Polly had decided to paint for her father a portrait of his beloved dog, Rufus, and while the dog had been content sleeping in the sun for some time, now that her mother had entered, he was bounding about the room excitedly. Polly had managed to sketch the dog over a series of days, and she was determined to get his shading just right.

"Off with you, Rufus," her mother said, shooing the dog out the door before turning to her daughter, her hands now firmly on her hips. "Now Polly, will you set that paintbrush down?"

Polly sighed, then paused and, setting her head to rights, looked up inquiringly at her mother. She could not imagine what this news was, given that they had been in the country living a rather boring existence ever since the weddings of her two siblings. First, her sister had been married, followed shortly thereafter by her brother, Benjamin. *That* had rather shocked Polly. She had thought Benjamin would never settle down. So, too, had her mother, who had seemed utterly relieved that Benjamin had found a wife, and one who seemed to be able to keep him out of trouble, a task Polly had always imagined to be impossible.

"You are to have a brand new wardrobe!" her mother declared, excitedly clapping her hands together. "Can you believe it?"

The paintbrush fell from Polly's hands as she stared up at her mother, excitement now beginning to swirl through her.

"The Season is soon to be upon us once more and, since it is now almost a year since your older sister married, it is high time that you find yourself in a similar situation," her mother continued, twirling around the room as though it was she who was about to throw herself headlong into the whirlwind of London society in order to find herself a husband. "Once in London, Madame Dubois will come visit and outfit you in the finest of fashions! You do know how she is always aware of the latest styles straight from Paris."

"Madame Dubois is not actually French, Mama. She just pretends to be so."

Marie waved her hands in the air as if to say it didn't really matter.

"They all do, darling. Most of the *ton* uses her, so it matters naught to me whether she is from the streets of St. Giles, so long as I can trust she will make sure you are noticed by all. We must get ourselves ready, however, for our time to leave will come quickly. We are to leave in two days."

"In two days," Polly breathed, her hand covering her heart, "oh, Mama!"

As the Duke of Ware's youngest daughter, Polly had long been waiting for her turn to look for a suitor, ready to take the next step in life. After Violet had married, Polly had been forced to return home with her mother and father, knowing that she would have to wait for the following year's Season before she could return to London.

She and her mother had wanted to return to the city for the 'Little Season' during the winter months, but the snow had caused the roads to become barely passable, meaning her father had decided it best they remain at home. The long winter had dragged at times, for Polly no longer had the company she was used to. Her oldest brother, Daniel, was still unmarried, but preferred his own London home and was hardly ever present at society events. The rest of her siblings had all settled into lives and adventures of their own while she lingered at home, lost in dreams of whom she might, one day, fall hopelessly in love with.

A dream that might finally soon be fulfilled.

"I have already sent a maid to help Lucy pack your things," her mother smiled, her eyes sparkling. "Your father is to come for a short time, but will return home within a sennight, leaving both us in London for a time. You know how much he has to do."

Polly, her painting forgotten for the moment, felt like dancing across the drawing room, already caught up in all that might come her way. "Oh, Mama! How wonderful!"

"We already have an invitation to Lord and Lady Gregory's ball next week, so we must ensure that you have at least one new gown by then." Her mother's expression softened as she reached across to take Polly's hand. "I mean to do the best for you, my dear. No expense will be spared, I promise you that. We shall make sure that you are happy and settled by the end of the Season."

With a wide smile blooming on her face, Polly could not help but allow hope to blossom in her heart, even though she knew it had taken her sister Violet more than a few seasons to find herself a match. Violet, however, had rather particular notions about gentlemen of the *ton*, while Polly was convinced it would not take nearly as much time to find the man of her dreams.

"Oh, I do hope so, Mama. I can hardly wait." Even if she did require more than one season, however, she didn't much mind. She would never admit it to her mother, but she was just as excited to be in London society as she was to find a husband.

"Just as it ought to be," her mother replied, with a nod, a satisfied smile set on her face. "Finally, a child of mine who understands I want only what is best. You are young and more than pretty, as well as the daughter of a duke. Your dowry is sizeable, and now your wardrobe should not be bested by any other young woman. You shall have men dancing all around you, desperate for your company, I promise you that."

Getting to her feet, she smoothed her dress and then came over to Polly and kissed her lightly on the cheek. "Now, I must go and see that all is being done as I asked." She picked up Polly's paintbrush and handed it back to her, so thrilled about her upcoming plans that she didn't seem to notice the drop of paint on the floor, which Polly surreptitiously tried to cover with her slipper. "I will see you at dinner, my dear."

As her mother let herself out of the room, Rufus, who had been waiting at the door, came bounding back in. Once Marie had closed the door firmly behind her, Polly let out a rather loud squeal of delight and, clasping her hands together, rose to her feet and began to dance around the room, Rufus now chasing her excitedly. As he jumped up, she grasped his paws in her hands and pretended to dance, until he barked to be let go.

Finally, *finally*, the attention was to be on her alone. Her mother would no longer be looking out for gentlemen for Violet, nor a wife for Thomas or Benjamin. As she had all but given up on Daniel's marriage prospects, now her attention would be entirely fixed on Polly. Violet had despaired of her mother's constant presence, as they always seemed to be having words, but Polly didn't mind it. Her parents' marriage had been arranged for them, and they had always been happily in love.

Her heart beating wildly with delight, Polly looked out of the window at the familiar view. The rolling hills and small cottages would soon be replaced by the grand, yet tight buildings and bustling streets of London. No longer would she spend days and nights with only her mother for company, forced to remain indoors while the wind and the rain beat down wildly against the windows.

"Mayhap I shall never live here again," Polly whispered to herself, ignoring the slight twinge of sadness that hit her soul with that thought. "Perhaps I shall soon be mistress of my own home."

While she had been to London before for the Season, she had never truly allowed herself to do anything more than further certain acquaintances, for she had known her father expected her older sister Violet to marry first. A sense of freedom filled her as she drew in a long breath, her smile broadening. Now if a gentleman should ask to take her for a ride in his phaeton, she would be free to accept.

Violet, of course, had been much too careful when it came to gentlemen, although Polly was glad that her sister had managed to find so kind a husband. However, Polly had always found Violet far too wary of gentlemen's intentions, worrying that they cared only for her father's title and status as opposed to her heart. Polly had no such fears, for surely she would be able to tell if someone truly cared for her, would she not? Polly prided herself on being a rather excellent judge of character, and she would know if a gentleman's whispered words of love were true.

"Two days," she whispered, her breath frosting the window, "two days and I will be back among society."

She could hardly wait.

* * *

Keep reading Hope of Romance!

ALSO BY ELLIE ST. CLAIR

Lady of Charade

The Unconventional Ladies Box Set

To the Time of the Highlanders
A Time to Wed
A Time to Love
A Time to Dream

Thieves of Desire
The Art of Stealing a Duke's Heart
A Jewel for the Taking
A Prize Worth Fighting For
Gambling for the Lost Lord's Love
Romance of a Robbery

Thieves of Desire Box Set

The Bluestocking Scandals
Designs on a Duke
Inventing the Viscount
Discovering the Baron
The Valet Experiment
Writing the Rake
Risking the Detective
A Noble Excavation
A Gentleman of Mystery

The Bluestocking Scandals Box Set: Books 1-4
The Bluestocking Scandals Box Set: Books 5-8

Blooming Brides

A Duke for Daisy

A Marquess for Marigold

An Earl for Iris

A Viscount for Violet

The Blooming Brides Box Set: Books 1-4

Happily Ever After

The Duke She Wished For

Someday Her Duke Will Come

Once Upon a Duke's Dream

He's a Duke, But I Love Him

Loved by the Viscount

Because the Earl Loved Me

Happily Ever After Box Set Books 1-3

Happily Ever After Box Set Books 4-6

The Victorian Highlanders

Duncan's Christmas - (prequel)

Callum's Vow

Finlay's Duty

Adam's Call

Roderick's Purpose

Peggy's Love

The Victorian Highlanders Box Set Books 1-5

Christmas

Christmastide with His Countess

Her Christmas Wish

Merry Misrule

A Match Made at Christmas

A Match Made in Winter

Standalones

Always Your Love

The Stormswept Stowaway

A Touch of Temptation

For a full list of all of Ellie's books, please see
www.elliestclair.com/books.

ABOUT THE AUTHOR

Ellie has always loved reading, writing, and history. For many years she has written short stories, non-fiction, and has worked on her true love and passion -- romance novels.

In every era there is the chance for romance, and Ellie enjoys exploring many different time periods, cultures, and geographic locations. No matter when or where, love can always prevail. She has a particular soft spot for the bad boys of history, and loves a strong heroine in her stories.

Ellie and her husband love nothing more than spending time at home with their children and Husky cross. Ellie can typically be found at the lake in the summer, pushing the stroller all year round, and, of course, with her computer in her lap or a book in hand.

She also loves corresponding with readers, so be sure to contact her!

www.elliestclair.com
ellie@elliestclair.com

Printed in Great Britain
by Amazon

57803791R00116